Also by Dean Vincent Carter:

The Hand of the Devil
The Hunting Season

Dean Vincent Carter

Blood Water

CORGI BOOKS

BLOOD WATER
A CORGI BOOK 978 0 552 55573 9

Published in Great Britain by Corgi Books,
an imprint of Random House Children's Books
A Random House Group Company

This edition published 2009

1 3 5 7 9 10 8 6 4 2

Copyright © Dean Vincent Carter, 2009

The right of Dean Vincent Carter to be identified as the author of this
work has been asserted in accordance with the Copyright, Designs and Patents Act 1988.

The Random House Group Limited supports the Forest Stewardship Council (FSC), the leading
international forest certification organization. All our titles that are printed on Greenpeace-approved
FSC-certified paper carry the FSC logo. Our paper procurement policy can be found at
www.rbooks.co.uk/environment.

Typeset in Adobe Caslon Pro 13/16.5pt
by Falcon Oast Graphic Art Ltd.

Corgi Books are published by Random House Children's Books,
61–63 Uxbridge Road, London W5 5SA

www.**kids**at**random**house.co.uk
www.**rbooks**.co.uk

Addresses for companies within The Random House Group Limited can be found at:
www.randomhouse.co.uk/offices.htm

THE RANDOM HOUSE GROUP Limited Reg. No. 954009

A CIP catalogue record for this book is available from the British Library.

Printed and bound in Great Britain by
CPI Bookmarque, Croydon, CR0 4TD

This book is dedicated to Tenbury Wells.
Home is where the heart is.

PROLOGUE

Thursday 14 September

I managed to steal another hour in the laboratory tonight to examine the specimen before retiring to bed. I am beginning to understand that I have in my grasp something quite unique but potentially dangerous. I must keep checking my equipment to ensure everything is secure. If the specimen is as intelligent as I suspect, then it needs to be properly contained.

Holland is like a leech – he won't leave me alone, always asking what I'm up to, what my plans are . . . He hangs around like a bad smell. It's not like he has nothing to do, and the recreation room is full of books and DVDs. I wish he'd find someone else to pester. I doubt he knows what I'm doing though. I hope not. I get the feeling he wouldn't be able to keep a secret, especially one as important as this. It has become necessary to keep an eye on him at all times.

Friday 15th September

I introduced the specimen to a trout from the lake today. Incredible! I was dumbstruck and could do nothing but stare at it for several minutes. It entered the trout through its mouth and just disappeared inside. The specimen reminds me a little of a hagfish, or one of those ghost slugs that turned up in Wales last year and because of this I assumed it might attempt to eat the trout from the inside, but then the fish started to behave oddly. Its swimming pattern was erratic, clumsy, as though it was learning to swim for the first time. It would repeatedly attempt to leap out of the water. I had the impression that the fish was no longer in control of its body, and that the specimen was somehow in the driving seat.

The trout started to die after only an hour or so. Its colour changed dramatically and its life ebbed away. It was in an awful state – seemed to have practically liquefied. I wonder if the specimen infected it with something. The creature emerged from what was left of the trout and actually started to swim in the water like the fish, something I hadn't seen it do prior to its invasion. Had it learned? Had it absorbed information from the fish during its occupation? I'm going to try it on one of Sally's snakes later. It'll end in death for the poor creature, but Sally need not find out. It is in the interest of science after all. Perhaps the specimen will learn from the snake too and be able to imitate it. God, I can't wait to find out. I've never been so excited. I must remember to sedate the snake first in case it tries to attack the specimen. I must also see if the specimen can survive out of water, though I don't want to risk harming it at this exciting stage.

Amazing! Success. As I'd hoped, the specimen did indeed pull the same trick with the python. The gestation period was again brief, but when it emerged, it slithered along the snake's tank, just like its host would. I was stunned. What _is_ this thing?

Just before bed I noticed a shadow outside my room. It disappeared before I could discover its owner. It must have been Holland though. I should have words with him.

Saturday 16 September

Rain today. I didn't have any courses, but some of the others did. They cancelled them. Pointless going into the woods or near the lake in weather like this. Most of them decided to watch films in the recreation room so I managed to get some more time to myself in the lab. We have to leave the centre by next Thursday so the maintenance people can come in. I must finish my initial research by then in case anything is disturbed or broken while I am away. It is not normal procedure, but I may even try to sneak the specimen home with me. I'll be in trouble if anyone finds out, but I hate the idea of my work being interrupted.

I still have no idea where it came from, and my searches by the lake for more have been fruitless. I decided to confide in young James about my find, since he is the most trustworthy person here. I asked him to look for more examples of the specimen while I was busy with other work, but so far, he has had no luck. I might ask him to try again next Wednesday when he is back. Perhaps this creature is alone in the world. Perhaps there are no more.

Holland has a habit of bumping into me late at night and asking me about my day, making it clear at the same time that he already knows. What the hell is his problem? Has he been stalking me? I wish he would find something productive to do instead of bothering me all the time.

I can't believe it. The specimen has gone! I don't know how it could have freed itself – the container was sealed tight. My God – what if this thing gets into a human being? It could be lethal. If I find it,

I might have to destroy it. I don't know if it is safe to keep it here any more.

I am convinced Holland stole it. I haven't seen him for hours. Sally says he's locked himself in his room. I went and banged on his door several times but there was no answer. He has to come out sooner or later. When he does, there'll be trouble.

CHAPTER 1
Sunday 17 September

'Hey, Sean!'

He turned to see his brother James jogging towards him.

'How are you feeling, mate?'

'Yeah, not bad,' Sean replied, wiping his forehead with the back of his hand. 'It's pretty hot though – reckon some people will find it difficult.'

'Yeah. Lucky to have a break in the weather though. Would have been miserable if it had been raining again. The ground seems to have dried out a bit.'

They stood at the edge of the large green meadow by the car park, watching all the other entrants warming up and drinking the free water provided by the race organizers.

'Mum and Dad not arrived yet?'

'No,' James replied. 'They'll be here though. Dad wanted to finish painting the fence before they left.'

'Oh, OK.'

'I had a jog around the lanes earlier. Injury's getting

better, but the foot still isn't back to normal. Wish I was doing the race with you. I should have been more careful in that half-marathon.'

'I'd have only tried to keep up with you anyway. And that wouldn't have been a good idea.' They both chuckled.

Just then an announcement came over the public address system, calling for the runners to assemble at the start line.

'Right, well, better get over there. See you at the finish if you're sticking around.'

'Yeah, course,' James replied. 'Good luck.'

'Cheers, bro.'

Sean made his way through the crowd of other runners, some still stretching muscles and limbering up. He was starting to feel thirsty again, but knew there were water stops on the way, and besides, he'd run in the heat before and had no problems. Still, he should have had more to drink beforehand, it was common sense. He wandered into the middle of the large group and waited for the horn. Looking around at the other competitors in their different coloured running tops and shorts, he started to feel excited – and confident too. He hadn't done the annual Orchard Wells ten-kilometre run before, so although he knew the area well, he wasn't too sure of the route; however, he'd studied the map, and it looked like there were only a couple of hills to deal with.

The countdown began. Sean could feel the heat and the anticipation of the crowd around him. Everyone was quiet, tensed; then the horn sounded and they began cheering. Sean started his stopwatch and set off, running with the others when a gap opened. The group soon spread out further as the faster runners at the front moved ahead. As they left the meadow and surged across the car park, Sean turned to wave at James who raised his hand in return.

He picked up a little speed as they climbed the hill, ready to slow down if the ascent became too tough, but the ground levelled out and then sloped down. He found a pace he was comfortable with and stayed with it, keeping his eye on his stopwatch and the mile markers that cropped up along the way. Three and a half miles in, he reached the first big hill. He took it at a slightly slower pace, and was able to get to the top without too much trouble, his breathing heavier but not a problem. There was a water station there, so he grabbed a cup, drank half of it while still moving and poured the rest over his head. He was disheartened to see another large hill up ahead, but he tried to keep up the pace, reluctant to slow down and walk like many of the other runners. He pushed on, perspiring, panting, driving himself forward, until eventually the top of the hill came into view.

Five miles gone, the end was in sight, but Sean was

struggling. He was finding it harder and harder to stick to the pace he'd set himself, and his muscles were aching. He had forgotten to take on enough water, but he pushed on, determined to get to the finish without slowing down. He kept up with a runner in front, then pushed harder to overtake. His throat was paper dry and his running vest felt soaked. *I must be nearing the finish now*, he kept thinking, wondering how one mile could seem so long. He carried on, gasping, veering off course a little every now and then, until he saw the other competitors leaving the road and heading down a narrow tree-lined lane. *Great*, he thought. *About time.*

He decided to speed up now that the end was near, pushing his body as hard as he dared despite the pain in his lungs. He turned off the road and hurtled down the lane, trying to control his body at the increased speed. Suddenly something felt very wrong: his feet seemed detached, his body heavier and his vision cloudy. He felt like someone or something had hit him on the head and he swerved to the side, colliding with a loose iron railing, nearly falling, but somehow managing to stay on his feet. He heard the railing crash to the ground and a nearby sheep bleat in surprise, but there was no time to worry about that now.

He looked at his watch again, finding it hard to focus: this could be his best time ever. He had to speed up and use every last ounce of energy if he was going to make this race count. It was no longer a casual race, a bit of fun; it was everything to him, all important.

He emerged from the lane into the large field – a crowd of people were clustered around the finish line at the far end. His feet still felt like foreign objects, and he now realized how much he was weaving to and fro. Something was definitely wrong, and it was more than just exhaustion, but he was still ignoring it, pushing himself to the limit. To the spectators he looked like a drunkard, or someone staggering injured from a battlefield.

Thoughts swam in his head. He finally understood that there was a problem, but he had no idea what. He lurched on, seeing what looked like people running towards him. Was that James at the front? It looked like him. In seconds his brother was right in front of him, telling him to stop: he was still moving though, resisting his brother's attempts to halt him, but then it registered. He was in trouble. All at once a black car appeared next to him. Where had it come from? And Mum was there too now. James was telling him to sit down.

Then they were getting him into the passenger seat; the owner of the vehicle – a man he didn't recognize – was asking him if he was all right. He didn't know though, he couldn't really tell. They drove off to the other end of the field. He saw other runners finishing. Not him though. For some reason he wasn't allowed to finish the race. Voices merged into each other, his vision swam and he started to panic.

CHAPTER 2

Ten minutes later Sean was sitting in the St John's Ambulance tent, an oxygen mask attached to his face, his hair matted to his forehead by sweat. He'd had some water and cola to drink, but he was still feeling awful. At his request they'd escorted him to the finish line so that he could complete the race, but that had just made things worse. His vision was swimming; he couldn't focus on anything. His muscles felt stretched and like jelly, unresponsive. He looked at his arms and legs and barely recognized them.

He could remember little of the race now, and even less of what he'd done that morning. His brother and parents had spoken to the St John's Ambulance man who'd picked him up in his car. The initial consensus was that he'd succumbed to heat exhaustion. The insufficient levels of water in his body combined with the heat from the sun had starved his brain of oxygen. He'd dehydrated quickly, and the situation had just gone from bad to worse. He sat there inhaling the oxygen, removing the mask every now and then to drink some more cola. Apparently the sugar would help him recover, but he had felt like telling the St John's Ambulance man that he wanted to go to hospital. None of the people around him had any idea how bad things really were.

Eventually though, after nearly an hour, he agreed to try walking to the car. Mum and Dad helped him, staying close in case he felt faint. They stopped by a mauve Vauxhall Astra, but when it became clear that this was dad's car, Sean panicked.

'What's wrong?' his father asked, seeing the concern on his face.

'Is this the car?'

'Of course it is,' Dad replied, almost laughing.

'I don't recognize it.'

'Come on, get in.' His dad opened the passenger door and helped Sean in. Mum and James got in the back.

Sean shook his head, looking around the vehicle, at the seats, the dashboard, the radio. None of it was familiar, none of it made sense. They left the car park, the other runners, the crowd of spectators and the sound of the voice over the public address system, encouraging the late finishers. As they drove through town Sean tried desperately to remember things, even the simplest things, but only fragments were clear; it felt as though his brain was collapsing, falling apart. His vision seemed stretched, and the sounds he heard as they passed people and other traffic were distorted, louder than they should be. *What if I'm going to be like this for the rest of my life?* he thought. *What if it gets worse and I end up disabled?* The panic rose, but he was unwilling to voice his concerns in case they became fact.

When they got home Dad helped Sean out of the car and guided him towards the back door. 'Everything will be right as rain soon. Come on.' He unlocked the back door and they all went in. Immediately Sean was hit by more unfamiliarity. The kitchen felt wrong. The table and chairs in the small dining area were also wrong – the tea, coffee and sugar containers ... the toaster ... completely wrong. It was as though someone had sneaked in while they were out and completely redecorated and refurnished. What the hell did it mean?

As if sensing his thoughts his brother said: 'Relax, mate, it's just the effects of heat exhaustion. Your brain's suffered a kind of attack and needs a while to get back to normal. This happens to a lot of people who've experienced what you have. It'll pass.'

'I hope so,' Sean replied, still finding the whole experience deeply unnerving. Part of him was convinced he'd been through some kind of time warp and had lost several months of his memory. That would explain why everything looked different. But that was crazy.

He managed to get upstairs without help and Mum ran his bath while he sipped a cool drink his brother had poured for him. Incredibly he started to feel better. He sank into the bath, letting his whole body relax, unmoving for several minutes until he heard his dad's voice through the door.

'Sean? Everything OK?'

'Yeah, Dad, fine.'

'OK.'

He heard footsteps fading away down the stairs.

Sean's vision was more or less restored, his muscles were now responding normally and he felt a lot better. After his bath he went into his room and lay on the bed. He closed his eyes, counted to ten then opened them again. Various things were still unfamiliar to him. The general layout of the room was right – the position of the door, windows and bed – but the bed seemed bigger, the duvet was completely foreign to him, as were his chest of drawers and alarm clock. He sighed, rubbed his damp brown hair, then turned onto his side and closed his eyes again. Maybe things would be better in the morning.

CHAPTER 3

Monday morning came and went, and Sean was surprised when he opened his groggy eyes to find it was already five past twelve.

'Bloody hell,' he said, rising onto one elbow; then, at a loss for anything more intelligent to say: 'Shit.'

He got out of bed, went to the bathroom, then stood on the landing, listening for any sign of Mum downstairs. She didn't work at the hospital on Mondays. Sean waited a moment or two, until he heard a cough and the sound of a newspaper being shuffled.

'Mum?'

There was a brief pause before: 'Yes?'

'I'm supposed to be at school.'

'I know but I didn't want you going in today,' Mum said, turning a page of the paper. 'Graham said you'd be better off resting for a day or two before going back. You need to take it easy. You gave your dad and me quite a scare yesterday.'

He thought about it and decided that he didn't

particularly want to argue with his mum's decision.

'Go back to bed. I'll bring you up some lunch in a bit.'

'Haven't had breakfast yet.'

'All right, I'll bring that up too,' she replied, joking.

'OK,' Sean smiled. 'Who's Graham?'

'He's the man from St John's Ambulance who looked after you yesterday. I know his wife, Jean.'

'Oh yeah.' He turned and went back into his bedroom, wondering why nearly everyone Mum knew seemed to be called Jean.

'And I don't want you out of that bed today, you understand? You nearly ended up in hospital yesterday.'

'Yeah, I know,' he replied. He knew only too well. He closed his door before picking up his copy of *Northern Lights* and getting back into bed. Pulling the covers over him and pushing the pillows up behind his head, he glanced at the image on the front cover. He didn't recognize it at all – it seemed different. He stared at it for a whole minute, trying to force himself to remember it, but it was no use. Why didn't he recognize it? Why was he still having problems with his brain? He tried reading, but he couldn't get into the book any more. Besides which, he was now developing a headache. He decided that since he was confined to his bed, he might as well sleep. So he did.

He awoke again at around one thirty, to an awful din

outside. It sounded like rain, but if it was, it was really hammering down. He got out of bed, went over to his window and opened the curtains to reveal a furious downpour outside. The density of the rain was incredible; the ground was already covered in water, tiny explosions from the raindrops making it look almost alive.

Sean heard his mum's voice from downstairs. She was talking to someone, on the telephone. When he turned back to the window he was shocked to see his dad below him, hands raised to the sky, smiling as though he was enjoying the deluge. But he should be at work now, Sean thought.

'What the hell . . . ?' he mouthed. He turned and ran downstairs to find Mum in the living room, staring out of the large bay window at the front of the house, the phone held to her ear.

'I know . . . I know, it's ridiculous. They said it would be big, but this . . . I know—'

'Mum,' Sean said, interrupting. 'Mum, what's Dad doing in the back garden?'

'Hang on a second, Barbara. What do you mean "What's he doing in the back garden"? Your dad's at work.'

'He isn't. I just saw him out the window. He's standing in the rain in the back garden.'

'What?' Mum just stared at him for a second before: 'Barbara? I'll call you back in a few minutes – is that all right? . . . OK. Don't you leave the house again.' She hung up and headed for the kitchen, Sean following close behind.

It was hard to see through the window. First Mum peered out into the garden through the window over the sink, then through the one by the dining table, but it wasn't long before she turned to Sean, shaking her head.

'He's not out there, sweetheart – you must have imagined it. Now get back to bed.'

'But I saw him, clear as day. It *must* have been him.'

'Well . . .' Mum went to the back door and opened it – 'Bloody hell!' – and closed it again. 'This rain is ridiculous . . .' She turned back to look at him. 'Do you want me to call him, just to be sure?' She went into the hall and picked up the phone. 'I'm sure he's at work,' she said as she dialled. 'It wouldn't make sense . . . Ah, Rob, are you at work? . . . Oh, it's nothing – it's just that Sean thought he saw you in the garden . . . Yes, I know, I told him that . . . Yes, I know . . . All right, don't worry about it, I'll see you later.' She hung up and replaced the phone in its dock. 'You see, I told you he was at work.'

'But—'

'Get back to bed, now! Come on.' Sean's mum ushered him back up the stairs, ignoring his protests. 'You get some sleep and stop worrying. You're just having hallucinations. You need time to recover properly.'

'I don't want to go back to sleep, I've slept enough.'

'Well, read your book then, or watch television.' She guided him up to his room and then stood in the doorway. 'And don't worry about school – you can stay at home all week if necessary. I'm not having you going back until you're ready.'

'OK.' Sean climbed into bed and just lay there, feeling miserable.

'Oh, cheer up, it could be a lot worse. Now what do you want for lunch? How about some soup?'

He just nodded.

It was nice not to have to go to school, but on the other hand Sean had the feeling that he was going to get very bored confined to his room all week. He was in his last year of school, and was having the best time he'd ever had. Lessons were more casual, the teachers were less strict with them – probably because they knew they'd be out of their hair soon. He hated to think he was missing out on something.

Outside, the rain had eased temporarily. He picked up the remote for the TV and turned it on. He found a weather report and saw a map with several red symbols indicating severe weather warnings. He wondered how bad the rain really was, and if they would have another flood like the one a few years back. The report ended, and as there were no other programmes on that he was prepared to watch, he shifted down to the end of the bed and switched on his games console. He was in the middle of a game called *Undead Platoon*, in which the player took on the role of a zombie soldier. His mission was to help his unit fight their way through a post-apocalyptic landscape and stop a madman from unleashing a deadly virus that would kill off all life on the planet, including the oppressed zombies. The unit was led by a rather unpleasant character called Sergeant Maul, who yelled orders and insults at the player if they were doing particularly badly. Sean loaded up his saved game and continued playing – until he was killed by a shell from an unseen enemy tank.

'Damn!' He dropped his controller on the bed beside him and watched as the ghastly decaying face of Sergeant Maul filled the blood-soaked screen.

'I did not give you permission to lie down, you maggot! Damn! Dying once is bad enough . . .' the soldier said, his voice fading. 'Dying twice is inexcusable.' And then the familiar words GAME OVER appeared on the screen, sealing Sean's failure.

He sighed and put down the controller. He was bored already. Maybe he should go back to sleep until Mum brought his soup up. Maybe when he woke the rain would have stopped and she would let him go outside for some fresh air. He wriggled under the covers and closed his eyes.

The next thing he was aware of was the sound of

bombs, machine-gun fire and the screams of dying men. He opened his eyes to find that he was lying on the ground, staring up at a night sky illuminated by flashes and explosions. The noise all around him was deafening and made his head hurt. He tried putting his hands over his ears, but he couldn't seem to move them; all he could do was lie there, wondering what on earth had happened. Then, amidst the cacophony, he heard the sound of heavy boots stomping across the ground towards him.

'Just what in the hell do you think you're doing, soldier? Did I say you could take a nap? Get on your feet before I tear you a new one!' A face came into view. An angry, ugly face, almost green in colour, pockmarked, scarred and wasted. There were no lips. One eye was missing, and in places the skull beneath showed through. 'You're a disgrace to this platoon! I ought to stuff you into a body-bag myself and ship you back with all the other lumps of useless meat. You make me sick! You hear me? You make me sick!'

Sean opened his eyes to find himself back in bed, but the sounds were still there. Then as his senses returned to some kind of order, he realized that the noise was different. It wasn't gunfire or the sound of exploding shells, it was the rain again, and it sounded just as insistent as before. He turned over and looked up to see the decaying, putrid face of Sergeant Maul.

'You make me sick!'

'Aaaaargh!' He closed his eyes and braced himself for the next shock. He waited for what seemed like ages, shivering beneath the bedclothes, praying that when he opened his eyes again the horrible image would be gone. When he finally summoned up the courage to look again, the sergeant was nowhere to be seen.

'Bloody hell,' he said, gazing around the room before focusing his attention on the downpour outside. 'I can't take any more of this.' He looked at the clock – almost four – then got out of bed and headed downstairs.

His mum was sitting on the sofa, a magazine on her lap, once more talking into the phone. She hung up and looked at Sean questioningly.

'I thought I told you to stay in—'

'I can't,' Sean protested. 'I keep freaking out.'

'What do you mean?'

'I keep seeing things . . . I just don't want to stay up there. Can't I just watch TV down here for a bit?'

'I suppose so. At least I'll be able to keep an eye on you. I brought your soup up earlier but you were fast asleep. I didn't want to wake you. You can put it in the microwave when you're ready.'

The only things on TV were boring discussion programmes, soaps and quiz shows like *Brainbox*, Mum's favourite, but Sean didn't really mind. He didn't want to be alone in his room any more. It was having a bad effect on him. He occasionally turned to the window to see how the rain was doing; just after five it actually started to die down.

'Looks like it might be over,' he said.

'Yeah, but they've forecast more for tomorrow,' Mum replied, her attention on her magazine. 'That's when we'll get the worst of it apparently. I hope the river can cope. It's burst its banks before.'

'Yeah, that'd be bad.' But for some reason Sean actually found the idea of a flood quite exciting. And if he was off school tomorrow as well, he might be able to go and take a look. That's if he could persuade Mum to let him out of course.

Dad arrived home shortly afterwards, and while he washed his hands in the sink, Sean filled him in on the strange vision he'd had earlier.

'You saw me in the garden? What was I doing?'

'Just standing there in the rain ... Enjoying it from the look of things. It was like that scene in *The Shawshank Redemption*.'

'Ha ha. Well, that's not the sort of thing I'm likely to do, trust me.'

'I know, it's just ... It was so real, you know?'

'The brain can make you believe whatever it wants you to if it tries hard enough.'

'Yeah, but it's *my* brain. It's me . . . It should do what I tell it to. It's not some other creature.'

'Well, sometimes it can seem like that. It can rebel, do things you don't expect, don't want. It's the brain's way of telling you that something's going wrong, or that something has happened to it and it needs time to recover.'

'Mmm, yeah, I suppose. I can't believe all this is because I didn't drink enough water.'

'Yes, well,' Dad said, drying his hands on a towel, 'you'll know better next time, won't you? Graham said you were "severely dehydrated" and narrowly avoided heat exhaustion. People have had strokes after going through what you did.'

'Seriously?'

'Yep. So you'd better be careful next time.'

'Yes, he'd better,' Mum said, coming in to check on the status of dinner.

CHAPTER 4

Feeling lazy, Sean slept most of the following morning. After lunch the rain eased up a little, and by then he was desperate to get some fresh air; he felt like a prisoner. Mum would be home from the hospital at about three, so he had over an hour of freedom before she got back to insist that he should rest. He needed to get out, but he was also curious to see how high the river had risen. He put on his jacket, then his boots, opened the back door and stepped outside.

It looked like the end of the world had begun. Water streamed over the slabs in the back garden and large muddy pools had already drowned the flowerbeds. The sky was unbroken grey clouds. The weather reports had been right: this was really bad. *God*, Sean thought. *If it goes on much longer we'll all be submerged.*

Although the rain was definitely stopping, the water was taking a long time to drain away into the already sodden ground. Sean locked the back door, then turned and splashed his way to the gate, stepping onto the driveway and looking to see if there was anyone else around. Unsurprisingly, there wasn't. He crossed the end of the cul de sac and went down the small path that led to the main road, hoping no cars would race through the deep puddles by the kerb and soak him.

As he passed the hospital and the New Inn, he wondered how much damage the rain might do, and if it would be permanent. It wouldn't be the first time the river had burst its banks, but it had rarely reached the high street. If it did so now and flooded the shops and houses of Orchard Wells, they would be in trouble.

When he reached the petrol station he was able to see the bridge and the river, and what he saw made him stop and stare. The river was far higher than he had expected; it raged under the arches of the bridge and was no more than a metre from the road. The foaming muddy water swirled as it hit the bridge; large branches and foliage were sucked under the torrent to emerge in pieces on the other side. He'd seen the river high, but never this high.

He walked on and saw a crowd of people gathered by the bridge, marvelling at the spectacle. As he moved among them he watched them shake their heads and laugh or just stare at the water surging past. He looked up into the sky and groaned as the rain resumed; how long would it be before the water rose up over the bridge? It had already swamped more than half of the field on the side of the river he'd just left. On the other side, the town side, it was nearly up to the car park of the Bridge Hotel.

After Sean's eyes had taken in enough, he walked on over the bridge, and instead of continuing up the high street he turned and followed the path along the river, towards the park. He couldn't take his eyes off the raging water, mesmerized by the little whirlpools. Two women with small children passed him, the children giggling and whooping with joy at the swollen river, their mothers markedly less impressed. Sean looked up to see lighter patches in the sky. Perhaps the sun would make it through after all.

As he entered the park, he kept his eye on the river. A huge branch bobbed above the surface of the torrent as it was hurtled downstream. He watched it until it disappeared from view, then walked on, turning right by the pagoda, where the river met a stream. The stream was also swollen and muddy, the water rushing by. Then he saw something that made him slow down and stop. There was movement between the trees on the slope leading down to the water. It looked like someone on his hands and knees, crawling slowly up the muddy bank away from the swollen stream. He seemed to be in a bad way. He was drenched, hair and clothes dripping as he struggled up the slope.

Sean continued to stare, slack-jawed, at the figure

several metres below him. Finally he shook himself and started to stumble down the sodden slope towards the figure at the bottom. He didn't quite know what he was going to do when he reached him. It would be hard to help anyone up the wet, slippery bank, but if he left him and went to get help he might fall back into the stream. Sean held onto branches and tree trunks as he made his way down, terrified of losing his footing. When he was a couple of metres away he stopped. The figure was no longer moving.

The man was now lying face down on the muddy ground. Sean swallowed and started to shake. Was he dead? *God no, don't let him be dead!* But maybe Sean could still save him ... Just as he was trying to work out what to do, he heard a low, drawn-out moan; it grew louder and the man started to raise his head.

As he caught sight of the face, Sean's concern turned to shock, then repulsion and fear. The man's skin looked yellow, sagging and corpse-like. His eyes were bloodshot, and had what looked like blue specks in them, though it was hard to be sure from this distance. His eyes held Sean's for several seconds; then he coughed and vomited into the long grass. Sean backed away instinctively, his own stomach heaving at the sight of the man emptying his. Before turning away he noticed that the vomit was red, like blood. This man was in a bad way, and it was nothing to do with the flood. He was trying to stand up, but seemed to have lost all sense of balance: he swayed on his feet and toppled over again. Sean wanted to go down and help him, but all that stuff the man had brought up had put him off. He could smell it now too – strong, pungent, with a distinct metallic tang that could have been the blood.

The man was dying – Sean knew this instinctively. He attempted to get up again but just slumped back to his knees. He was clearly in great pain and struggled to speak. The words Sean could make out seemed meaningless. Then the man vomited again, this time violently and for a long time. Sean couldn't understand how anyone could hold so much in their guts.

Convulsions rocked the poor man's body. He glanced pleadingly up at Sean, shook his head, then his eyes rolled around and his mouth gaped open to give a low moan and a sound like a distant hissing. Sean could only watch in horror as something black and slimy wriggled out of his mouth; it slid out, then fell with a splash into the foul mess the man had just disgorged.

He rose to his feet, staring at Sean, and said: 'The ... the centre ...' before falling backwards into the raging water with a huge splash.

Sean was all set to rush to the water's edge to try and help the man out – but then he noticed the black slug-like thing move. In two minds, he glanced at the ferocious torrent and realized that he couldn't have saved the man anyway – even if there had been any life left in him. He looked down again – and screamed as the black thing started sliding, snake-like, towards him . . .

CHAPTER 5

Sean panicked and turned, scrambling up the bank to get away from the creature and back home as fast as possible. Then he could tell Mum and Dad what had happened and let them decide what to do. But would they believe him after the way he'd been behaving since the run? They'd think he'd imagined it all – and he wouldn't blame them. But that was something to worry about later; right now his main concern was getting home – it seemed the waters were rising by the minute. He managed to climb back up to the path, getting his clothes filthy in the process, then jogged away from the bank, past the pagoda, and back in the direction of the bridge, his breathing laboured and his mouth dry. He had to stop for a moment or two when a throbbing began in his head followed by a wave of nausea.

The pain reminded him a little of what he had suffered just after collapsing at the end of the race. Then, it was due to dehydration, but now it had to be something else.

Perhaps he still hadn't fully recovered from the ordeal. He leaned over, his hands on his knees and took several deep breaths. Images flashed before his eyes – the course, the other runners, the iron railing flying towards the grass, the black car, Mum and James rushing towards him, concerned, and the oxygen mask going over his mouth time and again until he began to feel better. Dizziness came and went, as did the pain, and it was several minutes before he could think clearly again.

He stood up straight, looked at the park around him and was suddenly overcome with a sense of dread about what he'd seen by the edge of the stream – had any of it actually happened? Against his better judgement he walked briskly back and looked down the slope towards the water. He couldn't tell from where he stood if there were any marks in the mud – there were no signs of vomit. But he wasn't prepared to go back down, so the doubt would have to remain for now. But could he really have imagined it all? It had all seemed so vivid. The sight, the sound, the smell. Weren't a lot of dreams convincing though?

He gave up worrying about it and made his way back down the path. A figure carrying a large black umbrella was approaching, head down so that Sean couldn't see his face properly. As he drew closer, however, he recognized his form teacher. Mr Phoenix might be wondering why

Sean was outside in the rain and not at home resting, but it was too late to turn round or hide now.

'Sean?' Mr Phoenix asked.

'Hi, sir.'

'Shouldn't you be at home? I thought you were recuperating after what happened on Sunday.'

Sean didn't have time to think up a decent story, and he'd always found that honesty was the best policy with parents and teachers, regardless of the consequences. They always managed to find out the truth in the end.

'I was going mad in my room so I decided to get some fresh air before Mum got back. Wish I hadn't now.'

'I see,' Phoenix said. 'Well, you should probably head back before she catches you. Fresh air is one thing, but dehydration can really upset your system. You should rest.' He started to walk on, then stopped and added: 'What do you mean you wish you hadn't? Did something happen?'

'Well, I think I might have had a pretty vivid hallucination just now.'

'Really?'

'Yeah. I thought I saw a man crawl out of the river and fall back in again.'

'Are you sure it was an hallucination?'

'I think so. He looked like he had some disease or something. He vomited this black thing, then fell back into the river. It was mad, you know . . . It seemed real but . . . Couldn't have been.'

'Where was this?'

'Past the pagoda, down the bank by the stream.'

'Well,' the teacher said, looking down the path behind Sean, 'maybe I'll have a look just to be sure, but you'd best be getting home. I won't say anything about seeing you as long as you give me your word you'll stay indoors until you're back at school.'

'I will, I promise.'

'Good. Right, you take care then.'

'OK.' Sean set off, but a second later the teacher stopped him again.

'Sean!'

'Yes?'

'I forgot to warn you – the bridge is flooded now so you'll have to find another way across. Is there anyone who can give you a lift? Could be quite a journey.'

'The bridge is flooded already?'

'Yes. The river's still rising. I came down to take a look. I've already phoned the school to recommend sending everyone home early.'

'Oh, right . . . I'm sure I'll find a way to get back.'

'All right, but if you have any difficulty go up to the school, OK?'

'Yes, sir.'

'Right.' And with that the teacher walked on.

Sean adjusted his hood to protect his face from the rain, then hurried on along the waterlogged path.

When he reached the bridge, he was amazed to see that the water had swamped the road. It was swelling by the second, and was beginning to make its way up to the high street. He quickly headed for the video rental shop, where a crowd had formed. Cars had stopped on both sides of the river, the drivers staring, bemused, at the water, some unable to go either forwards or backwards. Just then, a police car arrived; two officers got out and started ushering everyone further up the high street. More people were stopping to marvel at the approaching tide. Some leaned out of windows; some interrupted their shopping to come and see what all the commotion was about. Somewhere a child cried out in excited glee.

The river was now a monster, a terrifying one, and it looked like there was no stopping it.

CHAPTER 6

Although he was worried about the flood, Sean's primary concern was getting home – it would be difficult as the only direct route from Orchard Wells' high street to the suburbs was now under water. There were back roads from the other end of town that would get him there, but it would take all day if he had to walk. He needed a lift. Then he remembered that his brother had said he'd be finishing college early today and might go for a swim afterwards. If so, his car would be at the pool.

Sean turned and headed up the high street, taking a left at the library, then over a small bridge that was dangerously close to the rising stream, and into the swimming pool car park. He scanned the vehicles. There were people chatting on their phones, no doubt informing loved ones of the situation. Others were getting into their cars and driving away while they still could. He checked each parking space, his eyes sweeping the vehicles, until he found it – a red Ford Fiesta with one hubcap missing. His brother was still there. He made for the entrance to the building and went inside.

Mr Phoenix scanned the path and the bank leading down to the water's edge for signs of disturbance; soon enough he came upon muddy footprints and trampled grass that he guessed had been left by Sean. He looked down through the trees to the brown, swirling water below, reluctant to go near it, but interested enough in Sean's story to see if there was any truth in it. The boy believed he'd been hallucinating after what had happened to him on Sunday, but maybe someone really had come to harm.

Mr Phoenix made his way slowly down the slope, using the trees for support when he slipped, but he soon reached the water and saw signs of a recent disturbance in the mud. It was hard to tell if anyone besides Sean had been there. He looked around for any sign of vomit, but could see nothing except... In the grass to one side he glimpsed something dark and slimy. He moved closer and looked down, trying to guess what it was. It looked like oil, only thicker, more viscous, and gave off an awful pungent smell. He squatted down to take a closer look but had to turn away as the smell of vomit assailed him.

Suddenly he saw movement in the grass on the other

side of the rough path: something was making its way towards him. He waited to see what it was – a rabbit, he guessed – but the grass stopped moving and nothing appeared. He walked over to the spot, crouching down to get a better look. In the thick tangle of grass and twigs lay something shiny and wet, long and dark – an eel perhaps. Whatever it was, he didn't really want to touch it, and he was about to leave it be when it shot out from its hiding place and attached itself to his face.

He cried out, more in revulsion than fear, and fell backwards onto the muddy ground, scrabbling madly to remove the thing from his face. It had contracted its body now so that it was shorter and fatter, like a slug, and though he pulled at it with both hands, it wouldn't come away. He yelled in panic as he felt it slide its way down from his nose and cheeks to his mouth, the smell making him gag. He didn't want it near his mouth, didn't want to taste it. He turned and crawled over to the edge of the stream, splashing water into his face in the desperate hope that it might remove the creature, but it was still sliding down and was now above his top lip.

'Urgh!' he cried. He got back to his feet, tried once again to wrench off his unknown attacker, then slipped and fell backwards into the water. The intense cold, the ferocious current and the incredible roaring force of the water claimed him.

* * *

Sean knew the boy working behind the reception desk at the swimming pool.

'Hey, Ed, is my brother still in the pool?'

'Nah, he got out about five minutes ago.'

'Ah, great, I'll wait for him.'

'Hey, Sean, is it true that the river's flooded the bridge?'

'Yeah . . . News travels fast.'

'Dad phoned. He said I should probably let everyone in the pool know.'

'Yeah. They'll have to go the back way up the hill. That's why I came to find James. I can't get home without him.'

'Oh, yeah. Why aren't you at school then?'

'Oh, long story . . .'

'Is it to do with the race?'

'Yeah. Still feeling a bit— Ah, here he is.'

James was coming towards the reception area. When he noticed Sean, he looked confused. 'What are you doing here? You should be at home.'

'I haven't got time to explain. The river's flooded, it's over the bridge and into the town.'

'Bloody hell.'

'Yeah, so we have to go home the back way.'

'All right, let's go. I've got to pick up some things from work. It won't take long though.'

As they went out into the car park, James took his car keys from his jacket pocket and looked up into the sky, which was still disgorging the seemingly endless rain. 'So why were you in town?'

'I had to get out for some fresh air. Thought I'd manage an hour or two before Mum came home.'

'But it was raining.'

'I didn't care.'

'So is the flooding really that serious?'

'Yeah.'

'Why didn't you go back over the bridge before it got so bad?' James unlocked the car and they got in.

'I was in the park and I . . . saw something really weird,' Sean said, buckling up his seat belt.

'Weird?' James started the car and checked his mirrors before driving towards the exit.

'Yeah. I saw this guy crawl out of the water – I don't know how, the current must have been really strong – but anyway, he crawled out, looking really bad, and puked this black stuff out and then just fell back into the water.'

'Are you serious?' James pulled out of the car park and headed up the hill past the small woodland path where Sean sometimes walked with his friends.

'Yeah, but I think I must have hallucinated it . . . I mean, it doesn't make any sense, it's mad. And I've been seeing some really strange stuff since the . . . you know.'

'Yeah, but what if you did see it? We should probably tell the police.'

'No, it's OK, I met Mr Phoenix from school when I was walking back to the bridge. I told him what happened. He said he was going to check it out.'

'Weird thing to hallucinate.'

'It wouldn't be a proper hallucination if it made sense though, would it?'

'I dunno. Shit, is this storm ever going to end?' The windscreen wipers were on full now, but the rain was so heavy that they were struggling to shift enough water to allow James to see the road ahead. 'If the bridge is already flooded and the river's coming up into the town, what's going to happen if the weather doesn't ease off soon?'

'I don't know,' Sean replied. 'But even if the rain did stop now, the shops and houses would still be flooded.'

They both shook their heads in bemusement.

'Maybe it's global warming,' James said. 'Or maybe it's just a freak storm.' He kept moving his head from side to side in order to see through the splashing of the wipers. 'This guy you saw . . . did he say anything?'

'Er, yeah . . . I think he said "The centre", or something. I don't know what he meant though.'

'The study centre maybe?'

It was only then that Sean made the connection

between what the man had said and the Lake Byrne Study Centre, where his brother worked part time. It must have been the muddled state his brain had been in since the run.

'I could check everything's all right there when I go in to get my stuff,' James said. 'You never know, they might be missing someone. It might be the guy you saw.'

'I really doubt it.'

'Why?'

'This guy looked like he should have died days ago. He was like a zombie or something. His skin was all yellow and his eyes were red. He had sores all over his skin . . . and no one should puke black stuff like that.'

'Jeez, I hope it really was an hallucination.'

'Yeah. This thing came out of his mouth too. It was like a massive slug or a snake or something. Really gross. Made me turn and run.'

'I'll bet. Well, maybe we'll find out whether what you saw was real when we get to the centre.'

Sean didn't like the idea. He didn't want to find it was real. He wanted to believe he'd imagined the whole terrible thing.

CHAPTER 7

A universe of water. The sound was what shocked him most. Above the roar of the current and his own thrashing limbs, there were other sounds – sounds he couldn't place – sounds that didn't seem to make any sense. He didn't know how much oxygen he had in his lungs but it was surely not enough to keep him alive for more than another minute or so. If he'd had more of a warning, he might have been able to take a bigger breath. He refused to believe it didn't matter any more, that it was irrelevant now. If only he could reach the bank and haul himself out of the raging force that had engulfed him ... But that wasn't his only concern. The thing that was fastened to his face was now moving down over his top lip. He had no idea what it was, or what it wanted, but he wished it would go away.

His lungs were heaving, the pounding in his head was increasing, but he became aware of the bank to his left. As luck would have it, the current seemed to be pushing him towards it; as it came close, he reached out and grabbed a tree root, anchoring himself to it, then pulling himself upwards with every ounce of strength. Up and up, and all at once the dull roar was gone, air and sound exploded around him and he sucked in a huge lungful of air, then another and another; then the water rose up and he got a mouthful of it.

Suddenly the black slug-thing shot into his mouth, making him choke, then clutch his throat; he lost his grip on the root and was pulled back under the water. As he twisted and turned beneath the surface, trying simultaneously to swim to the side and reach into his mouth to find the slug, a strange feeling came over him: a fuzziness, a wave of confusion and something utterly foreign. There was an awful, alien sensation of something moving about in his head, as if someone had reached in a hand and was rummaging around. He was paralysed now, unable to struggle, unable to do anything but drift down towards the river bed, his eyes open, staring, disbelieving, muddy water gushing into his lungs. His head felt like it was expanding, ready to burst at any second from the pressure. Incredibly, however, he didn't feel like he was dying. Quite the opposite in fact.

The rain let up a little, and James no longer felt he was going to crash at any moment. He slowed down, realizing the lane that led to the research centre would be coming up soon, and kept his eyes on the road ahead. Sean saw it before he did – a huge stretch of water that had collected across the road at the bottom of the hill; it looked deep enough to swallow them whole. James slowed the car further and stopped just short of it.

'Great. Now what do we do?'

'We've got to go through,' Sean said.

'We could get stuck though . . . Engine could get flooded.'

'We can't go back. This is the only way to get home.'

And then, to limit their choices even further, a van drove up behind them, blocking their retreat.

'Oh well,' James said, glancing in the rear-view mirror. 'Here we go.' He eased the accelerator down very gently and the car started to move forward. At first everything seemed fine: the water wasn't particularly deep, but then the car seemed to dip down. Sean caught movement to his left, and saw a small grey creature, possibly a squirrel, dart up into a tree beside the road. His head throbbed, and as he looked ahead again he was horrified to see that the water was now rising over the top of the car. He cried out to James, who looked at him as though he'd gone mad.

'What's wrong?'

'What do you mean "What's wrong"? We're under water! Look!'

James didn't seem to understand why Sean was panicking. 'It's not that deep.'

'Not that deep? Are you mad?' Sean could see floating detritus in the water – leaves, bits of twig, even a crisp packet. Bizarrely, a large fish passed by, gazing through the windscreen at them before swimming on. And then, in an instant, the scene dissolved away and they were no longer submerged but driving through the flood as before.

Sean shook his head. 'Sorry,' he said. 'I imagined it . . . I'm sorry.'

'Jesus, bro, the sooner we get you back home the better.'

James drove on slowly, still worried that the engine might become swamped and give up. Sean looked behind to see that the van was still there, the driver no doubt waiting to see if they made it through before committing himself. Suddenly the water dropped away, and the car was emerging from it. James accelerated carefully. Minutes later a sign for the Lake Byrne Field Study Centre appeared. They soon reached the small car park, and James swung into his usual space. There were quite a few vehicles parked nearby, though they could see no signs of life and no lights shone inside the building even though it was very gloomy.

'So what exactly do they do here?' Sean asked. 'You never really said.'

'Oh, you know, we do courses on wildlife and lake stuff,' James replied.

'Who are the courses for?'

'Anyone. We do special weekends for members of the public, but we also do research on the fish in the lake too. That's what I've been helping out with— Hey,' James said, rushing on ahead of Sean. 'The door's open. That's not right.'

They called through the open door to see if anyone was around. No answer.

'Doesn't look like there's anyone in,' Sean said. 'What should we do?'

'Well, we can't just stand here and get wet.'

'What if something's happened though?'

'Like what?'

'I don't know—'

Suddenly there was a sound like breaking glass from somewhere inside the building.

'Come on,' Sean said, starting to turn away. 'I don't like this, let's—'

Another crash of glass. They stood there, unable to move. Finally James pushed the door further open.

'I don't think we should go in,' said Sean.

'Someone might be hurt.' James clearly expected him to follow.

Sean had no reply to this, but he still didn't want to go inside. He had a really bad feeling about the place, but out here he was growing colder and wetter by the minute. He had to get under cover, and if James was determined to go in, maybe it would be all right.

CHAPTER 8

It seemed somehow colder inside than out, and darker too. The rain had penetrated the building, but not enough to flood it; the floor was covered with only a thin layer of water. They walked into the reception area and saw a large notice board with posters and leaflets pinned to it – *Walks with Wildlife* and *Discover Algae with the Expert* were displayed amongst others detailing more courses and activities. However, it was clear that nothing was going on right now: the place was deathly quiet.

Sean followed James along a corridor, then into a long room that looked like a laboratory. At first everything seemed normal, but as they moved through to the far end they saw smashed test tubes and other equipment littering the floor.

'What happened here?' Sean asked, taking care not to tread on any glass.

'Don't know,' James said. 'This is weird. I've never seen anything like this before. The caretaker usually keeps this place spotless, and everything was fine when

I left last Wednesday.' He went across to a whiteboard, which had recently been rubbed clean. In front of this was a desk covered with sheets of hastily scribbled notes and what looked like chemical formulas.

'What's all that?' Sean came and stood beside his brother, peering down at the notes. The two words that seemed to crop up more than any others were 'specimen' and 'host' – though the handwriting was often illegible: perhaps the writer had been in a hurry.

'Must be important if they were rushing to write it all down.' Sean picked up one of the pages and tried to read the scrawled text.

'It looks like Dr Morrow's handwriting,' James said.

'Who?'

'He's one of the scientists here. I help him out with his research from time to time.'

'What sort of research?'

'Oh, just ... stuff. You know. Lake stuff. This, though ...' he said, leafing through the papers. 'This is strange ...'

A word written in red capital letters on some lined paper caught Sean's attention: DANGEROUS. He pointed it out to James. They looked at each other in bemusement, then both felt a chill – as if they were no longer alone.

'Did you hear something?' James asked.

'No, but I think ...'

They turned round slowly and saw a figure in the

doorway. A bearded middle-aged man was watching them; his white lab coat was smeared with what looked like blood, and in one hand he held an axe. His expression was blank. Sean watched his shoulders rise and fall as he breathed, and wondered if he was mentally ill. Then the man spoke.

'James ... Sorry, I thought you were ...' It was a whisper, a painful rasp. 'Don't go.' The man seemed to come to life now. He slowly lowered the axe and leaned it against the door frame before coming forward as if hoping they wouldn't notice it.

'Dr Morrow?' James had been working with the scientist for several months, but he looked very different now – tired and drawn.

'What's going on here?' Sean asked.

Morrow approached them slowly. He seemed in no fit state to pose a threat, so they remained where they were. He looked briefly at the notes on the table, his eyebrows raised, then shook his head.

'It's gone.'

'What has?' James asked.

For a while there was no answer, then: 'The specimen.'

'Specimen?' Sean asked.

'Yes. It's gone.'

'No,' James said. 'How? What happened? Where's everyone else?'

'Everyone else?' The man looked directly at him now,

as though seeing him for the first time. 'They're dead. They're here, but . . . they're dead.'

James exchanged a worried look with his brother.

'For some reason it went crazy.'

'What is it?' Sean asked.

'It's an organism I discovered lying dormant in a pool near the lake a few days ago. I couldn't identify it – it appeared to be a type of sea slug, but after further study it became clear that it was a new form of life entirely. I dedicated all my time to examining it. Imagine my surprise when I found that it could enter the bodies of other animals and control them, even learn from them. But it seemed restless; it didn't like being kept here. All it needed was some idiot to come along and set it free. And that's exactly what happened. Holland became infected. I wondered if the specimen could take control of a human being, but I . . . I never wanted it to happen. Oh, God.'

'Infected?' James really didn't like what he was hearing, and neither did his brother. Sean was remembering the incident by the bank of the swollen stream, and was beginning to wonder if it had been real after all.

'The specimen got inside Holland's body. It was able to make him do anything it wanted. I locked myself in my room when I saw what it was doing to him. He killed the others in a terrible rage, then stormed out. I waited until I was sure it was safe, then came out.'

'He didn't come after you?' Sean asked.

'No. Thank God.'

'This all sounds so . . .'

'Insane? Yes, it does, but that's because this thing is something no one has had to deal with before. This is a new life-form, or at least one we haven't identified yet.'

'I think I saw this Holland guy,' Sean said. 'By the stream in the park. He looked terrible, like he was really ill—'

'What? You've seen him?'

'I think so.'

'How did he get there? Unless . . . The river.'

'What about it?' James asked.

'While that thing was inside him Holland kept screaming the word "home". Perhaps it made him go back to find the pool where it had come from. You . . . You didn't approach him, did you?'

'No. He mentioned the centre. I think he might have been trying to tell me where he came from. Then he slipped back into the water. Although before that he was violently sick, with blood and everything, and the . . . that thing fell out of his mouth.'

'The specimen? Perhaps it left his body because he was no longer of any use . . . I can't think of any other reason why it would leave its host.'

'I saw it move. It was disgusting. How did it get inside him?'

'The same way it got out, I presume,' Morrow said. 'Through his mouth.'

'Oh God . . . Mr Phoenix, my teacher, said he might have a look by the stream to check out my story . . . What if—?'

'We have to find your teacher and make sure he hasn't been infected. Where will he be now?'

'At school.'

'The High School?'

'Yes.'

Morrow and James exchanged concerned glances.

'There are hundreds of kids there right now,' James said, 'and this rain is going to cut the whole town off soon. They'll be trapped. If we go there we'll be trapped too.'

'No, no, the school is on a hill, isn't it? It might be cut off from the town but there'll still be the back roads. We should get there as soon as we can. If your teacher is infected, I can try and extract the creature before it does too much damage.'

'How?'

There was an uneasy pause.

'I have no idea. I'll have to work that out when we find it.'

Sean and James looked at each other, but in the absence of a better plan they followed the scientist out into the car park.

CHAPTER 9

It made no sense. When he regained consciousness he was already pulling himself up the bank. How was that possible? He was like a spectator inside his own body. He could hear himself gasping for air, could feel his arms and legs move as he scrambled out of the raging water, heaving his wet body with energy dredged from somewhere within. Moments ago he'd been drowning, dying. Now he was performing a feat of incredible strength – except it didn't feel like he was doing it. It felt like someone else was. He watched, perplexed, as his body continued to drag itself up the muddy bank, seemingly of its own accord, until it lay down on the ground and rested. He tried to concentrate on moving his right hand – pain lanced across his head. He moaned, although the sound seemed to stay inside, in thought form. He tried moving a foot this time – and again the same pain. It was as if there was a cold bar of metal inside his brain that throbbed every time he tried to do something.

What the hell has happened to me? he wondered. And then

he remembered the slug thing, and the way it had slithered into his mouth before he was lost in the floodwater. *Oh God. It couldn't possibly* ... He panicked, instinctively trying to get to his feet and run – as if that would do him any good. And he was in agony once again, and again he screamed soundlessly, this time retreating further back into his mind, into a dark corner where he could watch, hoping that somehow someone would set him free.

They ran towards the car to get out of the rain.

'I had no idea the weather was so bad,' Morrow said.

'The bridge is flooded. The water is into the town now. I've never seen it like this,' Sean told him. 'I don't know how the rain can last this long. There hasn't been a let-up to allow the water to drain away.'

'Looks like the specimen chose the perfect time to escape. So much panic and confusion.'

'Where did you find it, Dr Morrow?' Sean asked as he watched his brother struggle to get a clear view through the windscreen.

'In a small pool near the caves beyond the lake. It was dormant, asleep. I thought it was a rock at first, it was so hard. But when I picked it up it must have sensed the warmth in my hand and it just ... came to life. I don't know how long it had been like that, but some marine life can remain almost lifeless for years and years before reawakening.'

'Why didn't it infect you?'

'It was slow and sluggish to begin with. And unlike Holland I was careful. I'd never seen anything like it before so I kept it in a jar while I studied it, only taking it out when I wanted to see how it behaved with other creatures. I used a mask and handled it with forceps. It's funny, I thought the precautions I was taking were silly. I was treating it like any other animal when ... when things started to go wrong.'

'What other creatures did it infect?' Sean asked.

'Just fish and one of the pythons. I didn't have time to test it on anything else, but I imagine the results would have been similar ... If it was able to absorb information from those creatures – basic information like the way they moved – imagine what it could learn from a human being ... Although now I don't think I want to imagine that at all. Several good people have died. I would be quite happy to find that thing and destroy it, even if it is one of a kind. It's far too dangerous. Shame ... It could be one of the most important discoveries of the natural world ...'

'But human lives come first,' James said.

'Yes, exactly. Besides, we have no idea what its agenda is – if it has one.'

'Agenda? You mean it's not just killing for the sake of it?'

'I don't think so – at least not completely. When it was in Holland it seemed agitated, like it was looking for something. Maybe it did just want to go home. Maybe it killed them all because it was scared. God, what have I done?'

'It's not your fault,' James said. 'You had no idea this would happen.'

He drove as fast as he dared. Sean watched the road ahead for dangers. They came to two more floods, both times driving through carefully. Morrow stayed silent for a while, sitting back in his seat and thinking, perhaps formulating a plan.

The sky was growing ever darker and the rain was heavier, if anything. Sean kept thinking of the river water encroaching on the town, sliding hungrily towards the shops. It could already be seeping into ground-floor rooms, pouring into basements. What damage would it do if it was allowed to rise even further? The visions that went through his head were almost apocalyptic. He'd seen news reports of floods around the world: people on rooftops being winched up by helicopters, upside-down cars floating down rivers, buildings collapsing, possessions sinking or floating away for ever. It couldn't possibly get that bad here, but if the rain didn't stop soon, it would certainly cause devastation. He wondered if his own house was in danger. He didn't think so. They were quite a distance from the river, and higher up than the town, but . . . Horrible thoughts came into his mind, setting off his headache again.

CHAPTER 10

As they approached the town, they started seeing other cars. People were either leaving work early or collecting their children from school, knowing it might be impossible later. When they drove past the industrial estate, they could see more evidence of the rain's work. Even though they were on high ground now, blocked drains were spewing out water: there was simply nowhere underground for it to go. However, the driveway leading to Orchard Wells High School was clear, so James drove in and parked. They walked up to the new reception annexe. The receptionist, Mrs Evans, looked curiously at the scientist, asking his name and the nature of his visit but ignoring Sean and James – whom she knew.

'Yes, hello. My name is Richard Morrow. I'm from the Lake Byrne Field Study Centre. I, er ... need to see Mr Phoenix urgently.'

'Mr Phoenix ...' Mrs Evans checked her log book. Sean and James exchanged worried glances, wondering what they'd do if Phoenix was elsewhere or, worse, missing. 'I'm sorry, I don't have your name down here in the visitor's book. Are you sure your appointment was today?'

'Yes – no – look, I really need to see him right now – it's very urgent. Could you please call him?'

The receptionist merely checked the book again, as if to say *That's not how it's done around here, I'm afraid.*

Sean decided to have a go: 'Mrs Evans, it's really important we see Mr Phoenix. He found something of scientific interest and Mr Morrow needs to evaluate it. It could be very, very important.'

'Really?' She looked up. 'What did he find?'

'It's, er, a rare species.'

'A rare species of what?'

'We don't know yet.'

'All right, bear with me a second.' She sighed, shaking her head as she picked up the phone.

Pupils and teachers alike were leaving reception and heading out into the rain, beginning their journeys home. Sean had a feeling that for some of them it might already be too late; some were going to get stuck. He looked down the corridor and saw Mr Titus, the headmaster, conversing with two teachers and pointing in the direction of the main hall. He looked very animated and concerned.

'He's not answering his extension,' Mrs Evans said eventually, after being interrupted by several teachers and pupils asking about the weather conditions and travel arrangements. She hung up her phone in a manner that suggested she had more important things to do than chase errant teachers. 'He might have gone home already. I remember seeing him go out earlier, but not coming back. You could see if his car's in the car park, it's the black Honda Civic . . . By the way, Sean, aren't you supposed to be off sick?'

'I am. It's a long story. Thanks, Mrs Evans.' Sean then remembered that Mum would be home by now. He didn't have his mobile – he hadn't thought he'd need it on his walk – but James should have his. He would wait until they'd checked the car park, then get James to phone her with a plausible story for his disappearance.

With no other obvious course of action they went back out into the rain, scanning the cars for the one belonging to Mr Phoenix. James spotted it almost right away.

'There it is.'

'He hasn't gone home then,' Sean said. 'So he must either be here, or . . . he never returned from his walk.'

They stood there getting wetter and wetter in the rain, trying to decide what to do. Suddenly there was a flash of lightning, followed closely by a loud clap of thunder, and the rain intensified.

'This is ridiculous,' Sean said, the water dripping off his hood.

'Come on,' Morrow said. 'Let's get back inside – quickly.'

* * *

The rain prevented any part of him from drying out or getting warm. Not that he was concerned. He couldn't even feel the cold anyway. He was numb, devoid of sensation. All he could do was watch and listen as the thing controlling his body took him up the road to the top of the hill. Phoenix didn't know what the thing was planning to do with his body, and he didn't care, he just wanted it back. But he knew where it was taking him – that seemed pretty clear now, though he couldn't work out what it intended to do when it got there. He kept getting flashes in his mind – images of murder and mayhem involving people he didn't recognize. Were these memories? Things the creature had done while in someone else's body? He remembered the horrible pain he'd felt when he'd tried to regain control of his body earlier. The cold, searing sensation in his head was like an icy dagger. He knew he had to try again at some point, but the idea made him feel nauseous. Was he ill? Would it allow him to be sick? Maybe not.

There was a flash of lightning and a clap of thunder. The weather seemed quite appropriate for what had happened to him. Monstrous and terrifying. There was so much rain, so much water around. The road was just a river now, flowing back into the town. Had the thing inside him come with the flood? Maybe this was the end of the world. Maybe this was what happened when you went to hell. He coughed, though he hadn't meant to. Perhaps the thing had made him cough for some reason. Maybe it was still breaking in its new suit.

A noise came over the public address system. It sounded like someone had their hand over the microphone, but then it cleared and the headmaster's voice took its place.

'*To all pupils and members of staff. I have been informed by the police that not only is the main bridge over the river Teme out of service, but the roads leading in and out of town are flooded in several places. There have also been a number of accidents because of the weather, and it is very dangerous for anyone now travelling in a vehicle . . . or on foot for that matter. If you already have someone coming to pick you up, then please wait inside until they arrive. If, however, you normally walk home, then you will have to wait here until we have confirmation that it is safe for you to leave. The school buses left the depot but we don't know whether they will come here as normal. It's possible they may have to turn back, in which case some of you may have to stay the night here – or with friends who live nearby. Please don't panic, this is just a precaution. With the exception of those who are being picked up now, would all pupils, members of staff and visitors please go to the main hall.*'

'What should we do?' Sean asked.

'I think we should wait here to see if Mr Phoenix turns up,' Morrow said.

'But he could go anywhere, couldn't he?' James said.

'Well, yes, but . . . what else can we do? Waiting here is our only real option. And if he does come back we need to determine if he has the specimen inside him – although I'm not quite sure how we do that.'

'Yeah, but what if he doesn't turn up? I don't want to be stuck here all night. We should drive home while we still can . . . if we still can.' James still had his car keys in his hand, and looked like he was ready to leave.

'What if he does though?' Sean said. 'What if he does and that thing is inside him? There are hundreds of kids here. What if he goes mad and starts attacking them?'

'But if he isn't infected, then we've wasted our time and that thing could be anywhere,' James argued.

'God, there are too many "ifs",' Sean said. 'We're going round in circles.'

'Yes, that's right,' Morrow agreed. 'Let's just see if he does come here and deal with the situation then.' He sounded worried. Sean wondered then what he intended to do if he did decide Mr Phoenix was infected. How would he get the thing out when he knew so little about it? He also wondered how dangerous Mr Phoenix might be: the creature had killed several people at the study centre.

'You three will need to go to the main hall if you're not leaving now,' Mrs Evans said from behind the glass window of the reception desk. 'Before you do, though, could you sign the book?' She looked at Morrow. 'Sorry, it's procedure, especially at a time like this.'

Once Morrow had signed in he turned back to them. 'We should go to the hall then. That's where Phoenix will go when he gets here, I assume.'

They walked down the sloping corridor connecting the new annexe to the older building. Just then they heard muffled, tinny music, and James retrieved his mobile phone from his jacket pocket. He looked at the lit-up display.

'It's Mum,' he said.

'She probably wants to know where I am,' Sean said.

James answered the phone and began explaining the situation as best he could, trying to leave out as many of the bizarre details as possible.

'Yeah,' he said, trying to wind up the conversation as the three of them went into the hall. 'Yeah, Sean's fine, honestly. We should be home soon once we've seen his teacher. Mr Morrow needs to be sure he isn't sick. This parasite thing isn't contagious but it can do harm to whoever's carrying it . . . Sorry? . . . No, we're perfectly safe – don't worry. It's, er . . . not the sort of parasite that can go from person to person through the air, it's . . . a bit more complicated than that. I'll explain when we get back . . . Yeah, I'm looking after him – he was just going crazy stuck indoors, he didn't realize the weather was so bad . . . I know, I know, he's really sorry, but . . . No, neither of us knew it would get this bad. I think we should be able to find a back road home once we've checked out Mr Phoenix, but I'll give you a ring in a while to let you know what's going on ... I will, honest ... OK, bye.'

Although many pupils had already left, the main hall was still busy. Despite the situation the mood was generally upbeat. All around the room groups of people were deep in conversation: the flooding was generating more excitement than concern among the pupils, though the members of staff seemed genuinely worried. Sean saw some of his friends on the other side of the hall.

'I guess we just wait then,' he said, watching his brother and Morrow scan the room.

'Yeah,' James said, sounding almost bored. 'We could be in for a—'

He was interrupted by the loud voice of a teacher behind him: 'Nigel! You're drenched. Come on up to the staff room.'

Sean, James and Morrow turned and saw a woman – Mrs Rees, Sean thought her name was, though he couldn't remember what she taught – taking a bedraggled man by the elbow and escorting him back out of the room. He looked absolutely soaked, his hair plastered down, his clothes filthy, and his eyes somehow hollow and lustreless – but it was definitely Phoenix.

'God,' Sean said. 'He looks terrible.'

'The rain could have done that though,' James said.

'Perhaps,' said Morrow, moving through the crowd after the departing teachers. 'But we need to be sure.'

CHAPTER 11

They could have waited for Phoenix to get changed and return to the hall – but what if he was infected, and attacked someone? They had to check him before he had a chance to do any harm. As they left the hall, two teachers seated nearby stopped them and asked what they were doing.

'I have my car,' James said. 'I was waiting for my dad to text me to tell me the road home was clear, so we're going now.'

'Oh, right,' one of them said, eyeing Morrow strangely as the trio walked past.

They hurried back to the annexe. Morrow was humming a tune as if trying to calm himself down – and with good reason, Sean thought. He had already seen some terrible things at the study centre; perhaps he was preparing himself for more. Sean still had questions, but he'd have to wait for a more convenient time to ask them.

At the top of the ramp they waited for Mrs Evans to

turn her back before continuing past the reception desk towards the stairs that led up to the staff room.

'What now?' Sean asked.

'I must go up and talk to him,' Morrow said. 'Try to ascertain if he's infected or not.'

'But how will you tell?' James looked up the stairs as if expecting to see an inquisitive face at any second.

'Well, I don't know ... There might be a way ...' Morrow took off his glasses and rubbed the lenses thoughtfully. 'There could be physical signs. Sean, you said that Holland's skin was in a bad state, didn't you?'

'Yeah, but he'd had that thing in him for a while, hadn't he? If Phoenix has been infected it won't have been in him for long.'

'No, but still ... There may be signs. Perhaps his behaviour will give him away. I saw and heard what Holland did when he was infected. I might recognize some of that behaviour in Mr Phoenix, and perhaps I can stop him before he does anything terrible.'

'What sort of things did Holland do?'

'He seemed odd – it wasn't like he was under the influence of something, but as if he was ... someone completely different.'

'What do you mean?' James asked.

'Well, I think the creature takes control of the mind of its host. Don't ask me how.' Morrow stopped as his eyes were drawn to the figure at the top of the stairs. It was the woman who had escorted Phoenix from the main hall, Mrs Rees. She took a few steps down, then stopped, a curious expression on her face.

'Can I help you?' she asked, looking at them in turn, her eyes questioning, suspicious.

'Yes,' Morrow answered, before either of the brothers could. 'I need to speak with Mr Phoenix immediately.'

'I'm sorry, but he can't really see visitors right now. He needs to dry off and get warm. He got caught in the flood, and—'

'Yes, I know, that's why I'm here. I'm Dr Morrow, Mr Phoenix's GP as well as a good friend of his. He called me because he fell in the river earlier and was worried that he might be ill. I live nearby so I said I'd come and see him. He may well be fine, but it's probably best that I check, just to be on the safe side.'

'Oh, I see. Right, well, you'd better come up then, Doctor. I'm Mrs Rees, by the way. I teach English.' She turned and went back up the stairs.

Morrow told the boys to wait there for him; then followed her up to the staff room.

'What now?' Sean asked his brother.

'We'll just have to wait and hope Dr Morrow can determine whether Phoenix is infected or not. God I really hope he isn't . . . Not just for his sake, but because it means that creature is somewhere else then, and somebody else's problem.'

* * *

Upstairs, Dr Morrow was shown into the staff room. Phoenix was slumped in an armchair, his face averted, a mug of tea in one hand. He was drenched but didn't appear to be shivering.

'We should get him dry, shouldn't we?' Mrs Rees asked. 'He'll catch a cold.'

He could have caught something a lot worse than that, Morrow thought.

'Could I see him alone for a few minutes?' he asked, looking across at her.

'Well, yes, of course. I need to go back to the hall anyway. I'll come back as soon as I can.'

'Thank you, this won't take long. And he'll be fine.'

Mrs Rees nodded and turned to leave the room.

'Now then,' Dr Morrow said, approaching the seated man and already noticing a strange reddening of the man's forehead. 'Tell me how you feel.'

Without warning, the mug of tea dropped from Phoenix's hand and hit the floor with a thud, spilling its contents on the carpet. Then he turned his head to face the doctor.

CHAPTER 12

'Come on, boys,' Mrs Rees said to Sean and James. 'You'd better come back to the hall with me. The headmaster wants everyone together. Mr Phoenix will be all right – I'll check back on him in a while.'

'But we're looking after Dr Morrow. He doesn't know his way around the school,' Sean insisted.

'Yeah, and he said he wouldn't be long,' James added before Mrs Rees could get a word in. 'Just a quick look, that's all, then we'll bring him back to the hall.'

Mrs Rees thought it over. 'All right, but be sure you do. This storm isn't getting any better and we can't have people roaming around the school on their own. What exactly are you two doing here anyway? James, you left school three years ago, and you, Sean, you're supposed to be off sick.'

'I am, miss. I mean, I was, but I, well . . . It's a long story. We were on our way home when we got caught in the storm and we stopped to give Dr Morrow a lift. He works with James at the study centre.'

'Study centre? I thought he was Mr Phoenix's GP.'

'He is,' James said quickly. 'But he's also a marine biologist and runs courses.'

'He must be a busy man.'

'Yes, very busy.'

'All right, well, you may as well go on up to the staff room then. But don't let the headmaster know I let you up there. I'm trusting you two. Understood?'

'Yes, miss,' they replied in unison.

Mrs Rees still looked sceptical, but she left them to it.

'I can't believe this,' James said. 'It's like I never left school.'

'Never mind that,' Sean said, leading the way up the stairs. 'We can't leave Dr Morrow on his own with Phoenix if he has that thing in him.' They ran up the stairs to the staff room, and were surprised when they went in to find no one there.

'That's strange,' Sean said, scanning the large room with its sofas and coffee tables. On the floor a mug appeared to have been knocked over, its contents saturating a large section of the carpet. All was quiet.

'I don't like this.' James walked slowly towards the middle of the room. 'What's through there?' he asked, pointing to an open door on the far side of the room.

'I don't know,' Sean said, 'but I'd guess it's their toilets. That must be where Phoenix and Morrow have gone.'

'Yeah,' James replied, clearly reluctant to go and find out. 'I really don't like this.'

'Come on,' Sean said. 'It's probably fine.'

Above the sound of the storm outside, they suddenly heard a thud, a tinkle of breaking glass, and what could have been a cry. They both froze, then looked again at the open doorway, knowing that they had to go through it – even though it was the last thing on earth they wanted to do.

James went first, a step ahead of Sean, who was similarly terrified and readying himself to turn and run for his life at the slightest hint of danger. Ahead of them was a corridor and they saw doors to the ladies' and then the men's toilets, where James took a firm grip on the handle and slowly twisted.

It was an odd feeling – the kind of feeling, Sean guessed, that firemen must experience before opening the door to a burning room, or policemen entering a building where a criminal is lying in wait. It was something in the gut. As the door widened to reveal the broken window, the glass and the blood, they knew that something terrible had occurred.

They remained on the threshold, ready to turn and bolt, waiting for the inevitable shock. But if Phoenix was there, he was clearly in no hurry to move. He had to be out of sight in one of the cubicles. Either that or he'd jumped out of the window, but that would surely be suicidal. Sean wondered if anyone could survive the plunge.

'What do we do?' he whispered, hearing in his own voice that he was shaking.

James tried to reply, but nothing came out. He couldn't think of a good enough response anyway. And then the matter was resolved for them. There was a loud sigh, then a shuffling sound, and Phoenix came out of the last cubicle.

The three of them stood there, just looking at each other; rain blew in through the broken window and soaked the floor around them. Phoenix seemed to be grinning, but at the same time was clearly in some discomfort. Welts covered his face, red sores that certainly hadn't been there when he'd met Sean by the park. The man's eyes were bloodshot and looked like they'd receded, sunk back into his head. He shuffled awkwardly forward; a series of strange sounds issued from his throat before he managed to form words.

'You came with the doctor,' he said matter-of-factly.

Sean recognized the voice but it sounded strained. He and James exchanged glances and waited to see what Phoenix would do next: he scratched one of the angry sores on his right cheek, drawing blood, which trickled down to his chin. All three of them winced.

'Mr Phoenix?' James asked, wanting this confront-ation to end quickly. 'What happened to Mr Morrow?'

'What?' Phoenix noticed the blood on his fingers and rubbed it around. He looked up, first at the boys and then over his shoulder towards the window. 'Oh . . . he's outside.' He seemed to be in some kind of daze, or perhaps hypnotized. 'He's outside,' he repeated.

Sean swallowed, feeling the cold more and more. He looked at his brother for guidance.

'OK,' James said. 'You stay here for a moment, Mr Phoenix. Sean and I are just going out there to see if Mr Morrow is OK – we'll be back in a second.'

Phoenix just stared at them blankly, and they turned to leave, but then he said something that changed everything: 'He's got it now.'

The boys stopped and looked at him.

'What?' James asked.

'That thing . . . It's in him now. I'm . . . It needed someone fresh. I'm already finished. No use any more. I think the water did for me . . .' He coughed, turned and spat into the toilet behind him, then coughed again, violently.

'What do you mean?' Sean asked.

'It kept me going but I was ill, I think . . . From being under the water so long. I . . . God, I'm so tired. I need to sit down.'

'Why did it go through the window?' James asked.

'I pushed it,' Phoenix said. 'But it wasn't enough. That thing, it gives you strength . . . It seemed to make more use of my body than I could.' He coughed again. 'Except the head . . . I still feel dizzy.'

'Dizzy?'

'When it got me by the river I was staggering all over the place. I banged my head on a branch and blacked out. I didn't hit it that hard, but the creature went mad. I think while it was in my head it was extra sensitive to any pressure or trauma there. Any other part of the body doesn't seem to matter so much.'

'What does it want?' Sean asked.

'I'm not sure. It was looking for something but I didn't understand what. It has no consideration for life. It's cold. That's why I pushed it out of the window. You have to stop it . . . I really need to rest.'

'Did it communicate with you?' James asked.

Phoenix wiped his forehead, drawing more blood from the sores there. When he looked back at the boys he could see horror in their eyes at his appearance. 'When it was in me I could hear random, jumbled thoughts. I don't know what it is, but I sensed it was intelligent . . . And very, very tired of being lonely. Things are different now. Whatever it is after, it won't stop until it gets it.' His stare bored into each of the brothers in turn. 'There are more than three hundred children here right now. They are all in serious danger.' He coughed again, this time spitting a dark red liquid onto the floor. 'That thing has made me very ill. I think if it had been in me any longer I might have ... Please, I really do need to sit down.' Phoenix pushed past Sean and went into the staff room, where he collapsed into a chair.

Sean looked back at his brother, then turned to peer out of the window into the storm. The rain was still sheeting down and it was very gloomy now. However, it was clear that there was no body on the ground below the window.

'It's alive,' James said, turning to his brother. 'It's out there somewhere ...'

CHAPTER 13

Mr Waites, the history teacher, hadn't heard the head-master's announcement asking everyone to congregate in the main hall: the faulty speaker in his classroom still hadn't been fixed, and his radio was on. He wanted to go home, but if he didn't mark the test papers from the previous week now, he never would. He scratched his head and looked out of the window. The rain was still hammering down – he hoped the roads wouldn't be flooded. Most of the children should have left for the day by now, but even so, the school seemed unnaturally quiet. In a while, he thought, he would go up to the staff room to make himself a coffee; first he wanted to get two more papers marked.

But as he picked up the next exam paper, he had the unnerving feeling of being watched. There was no one in the doorway. Then, as he turned back towards the window, he knew, even before he had any evidence, that there was someone standing outside. Except that there was no one there. He got up and went across to the window, trying to see through the downpour. What kind of an idiot would be wandering about in that? He wondered if he should go and take a look, then thought better of it. Why get drenched chasing after some fool? It had probably just been his imagination anyway. He went back to his desk, sat down and resumed his marking, with no clue as to either the true extent of the flooding or the horrific events unfolding within the school.

'We need to tell the others,' Sean said. 'Quickly.'

'Tell them what?'

'I don't know, but he could be back inside already. We can't just let that thing keep jumping into people. Look what it did to Mr Phoenix – he looks terrible.'

They both turned back to the teacher, now slumped limply in his chair. They could only guess at the awful changes that had taken place inside his body – he looked near death.

'Sean,' Phoenix said weakly. 'Come here.' Sean went and sat on a nearby sofa. 'Sean, that thing has to be stopped. It's scared and angry. Whatever it wants, I have a horrible feeling something bad will happen if it finds it.'

'How are you feeling?' James asked, changing the subject.

'Bloody terrible,' Phoenix answered, coughing. 'It's

like a bad case of the flu. Everything feels tender and swollen. I'm bunged up and—'

'We'll get you to the hospital as soon as the weather eases a little,' James said. 'It's still too dangerous to go out now.'

'Come on,' Sean said, tugging James's sleeve. 'We need to tell Mr Titus and the others what's going on. We won't tell them everything. We'll just say that Dr Morrow's gone mad and needs to be restrained.'

'Titus'll think we're mad,' James told him. 'We should try and deal with this on our own.'

'But we can't. That thing's too dangerous.'

'Waites,' Phoenix said. 'See if he's in his classroom – he usually stays on after school to catch up on paperwork. If he's here he's more likely to listen to you than Mr Titus. Titus is such an idiot.' He coughed again.

Sean and James nodded, then turned and reluctantly left the teacher to go downstairs, wondering if Morrow and the thing inside him were already back inside the building.

'Oh God,' Phoenix whispered once the boys were out of earshot. 'What the hell is happening to me?'

Most of the pupils had already been picked up by parents, and incredibly one of the school buses had managed to make it through to collect the students – the driver said there was still a relatively safe route back to the depot twelve miles away. In the hall Mr Titus, Mrs Rees and the few remaining children were sitting or standing near the huge windows, watching the rain and the pools of water that had formed outside.

'It's just ridiculous,' Mrs Rees muttered.

'I dread to think what this is doing to the town,' Mr Titus said. 'Remember the floods we had before? It took months for some businesses to recover. Some of them never reopened. The cinema has been refurbished at least twice because of floodwater. It's amazing how much destruction can be caused by just a few hours of rain.'

'Yes, well, I hope it stops soon. I don't want to be stranded here all night. I'm sure the kids don't either. Right, I'd better go back to the staff room to check on Nigel. I'll be back in a second.'

Outside was a wall of water. Cold water. The creature inside Morrow was content to wait, at least for now, for the right opportunity to present itself. It didn't feel the cold like its host did, and it couldn't understand why he was shaking so much and making that odd sound with his teeth, but it realized that these human beings were afraid of being cold and wet. It could hurt them. So it wasn't going to stay outside for long – just long enough. It could feel that some of the man's bones had been broken. There was pain, but it buried this, kept it locked away so that it could concentrate. Luckily the injuries didn't impede movement.

It had already crept around most of the school buildings looking for signs of life inside, and so far had only spotted one person apart from the three it had left upstairs in the staff room. They had been sitting in a classroom and had been a prime target, but there seemed no point in changing bodies at this point, not while this one's memories hadn't yet been thoroughly plundered.

And it wasn't an easy task either. Morrow seemed to guess that the creature was looking for something, and was trying to block it, to hamper its efforts by thinking completely random and meaningless thoughts. It would learn what it needed to though. Whatever that was. And that was really the problem. It knew it had lost something at some point, a long time ago, but it couldn't remember what it was. Whatever it was, the secret wasn't in Morrow's mind, but he might still have a clue as to who did possess that knowledge.

What is it? the creature demanded in frustration within Morrow's mind. *What is it that I need to know?*

Although it was unaware of it, a moan issued from Morrow's lips. It was a moan of helplessness and distress – though it was completely lost in the dark and the rain. But the moan was less to do with Morrow's sorry state, and more to do with what he had seen inside the building. He recognized the woman. He'd seen her earlier.

His thoughts were in a mess, jumbled up and blurred. The entity in his head was clouding his memory as well as governing his mind. Then he felt it squirm. It had seen her too, and it made him move towards a point of interception. Morrow couldn't bear the thought of another helpless person being infected. *Please* – the thought, weak, drifted somewhere through his war-torn subconscious – *stop this now . . . Whatever it is you want to know, I can't help you. That woman, leave her alone. No more. Please, no more . . .*

Mrs Rees had half expected the head to chastise her for leaving Mr Phoenix unattended, but he was clearly preoccupied with the environmental calamity that was unfolding outside. She strode up the corridor towards the annexe and passed the reception area, now empty as Mrs Evans had decided to take a risk and drive home in the rain. She was about to go up the steps leading to the staff room when she heard the main doors open.

CHAPTER 14

In the staff room above, Phoenix coughed up blood for the third time. He'd been expecting as much, even though he knew little about what was really going on within him. His insides felt like jelly, his muscles were limp and barely responsive, and his eyes hurt. He was very thirsty too, so he tried to first sit, then stand up so he could go and get a glass of water. His stomach was instantly attacked by cramps and he doubled up in pain. He clutched his sides, then bent over and vomited dark blood onto the carpet, his eyes bulging in shock as he watched the cascade from his insides flow out of his mouth. The blood was specked with black dots and he wondered what was happening to his system – and what the creature had left inside him. He shook his head and started to panic. The pain in his stomach grew; he now had a splitting headache too. He staggered backwards and steadied himself against the wall before vomiting again, even more than before.

Afterwards Phoenix was overcome with dizziness, so

he fell back into the chair and waited, praying for the nausea to pass. But it didn't, it simply changed form, the waves of pain and sickness washing over him in unrelenting assaults. Blood was now seeping from his nose, and small cuts that had recently healed were now red and raw once more. He didn't know if he was more embarrassed or terrified by the fact that his trousers were now soaked through with something horrible.

Phoenix sobbed as the rest of his insides tried to force their way out.

Mr Waites was indeed in his classroom, as Phoenix had guessed. When Sean and James burst in, he jumped and had to steady himself on his chair.

'Bloody hell, don't you two know how to knock?' He put his pen down and scowled at them.

'Sorry, sir,' Sean said, 'but we need your help.'

Waites stood up. He was just over six foot, in his early forties – though he looked younger – fit and strong enough to put Mr Cole, the PE teacher, to shame. His hair was long and dark, and he wore small, round, wire-rimmed glasses.

'What sort of help? Is it to do with the rain?' Although he'd been too absorbed in his work to pay much attention, Waites now realized that the weather must be causing havoc.

'Sort of,' Sean said. 'It's a parasite.'

'What is?' Waites looked from Sean to James, whom he vaguely recognized as Sean's brother.

'It's something we found at the research centre where I work,' James told him. 'It can get into people and make them do things. It's got a mind of its own.'

There was a moment of silence before Waites took off his glasses, rubbed them on his shirt then put them back on.

'What the hell are you two talking about?'

'Dr Morrow, isn't it? Good lord, you must be drenched.' Mrs Rees was startled by the sight of the scientist standing, dripping, just inside the entrance doors, and approached him slowly, feeling that something was wrong. 'Are you all right? Where are the boys?'

She watched Morrow's eyes move from her to the staff room above, so she followed his gaze. When she turned back she was a little unsettled to see that Morrow was now closer, though she hadn't heard him move.

He opened his mouth to speak, then closed it again as Mrs Rees started to back away towards the staff-room steps. He followed her at the same speed, smiling now in a way she really didn't like. She was half expecting him to suddenly jump on her and pin her to the steps when he started coughing, then, after looking around frantically, dashed into the boys' toilets.

She turned and took the steps two at a time, glancing

back only once to make sure she wasn't being followed. When she reached the top she turned to see all that was left of Nigel Phoenix.

Morrow stumbled into the toilets, coughing and spluttering. His thoughts were churning again. He could sense the creature screaming in frustration and impatience. He had been telling it over and over again that he knew nothing, and he sensed it had finally decided to believe him. He didn't know what it was after, and suspected that it didn't either, but he was pretty sure he was holding no profound secrets. The creature had scoured his mind, seeing many things – Morrow retrieving it from the pool, taking it to the study centre, conducting tests on it – but none of this was useful: it was information it already possessed.

Morrow staggered towards one of the hand basins and felt his stomach heave. Then he felt a movement in his head, and something dislodged itself, then wriggled through impossibly small spaces to squeeze itself into his mouth, then out into the basin below him. He spat, stared at the black monster wriggling in the basin, then heaved and vomited all over it. It sprang up and managed to ooze up the spout of the tap, before contracting and squeezing its body so that it could work its way up into the spout and then into the plumbing system itself. As it disappeared, Morrow sighed with relief, but then his stomach turned again, and spasms of pain racked his body, and he knew his ordeal was far from over.

'I know this sounds like some sort of *Doctor Who* shit,' James said, 'but it's true, and we need to stop it before it infects everyone.'

'Infects everyone?'

'Yeah, Dr Morrow used it on a couple of animals at the research centre. It poisoned them while it was inside and they died once it had left them. It seems to have had a bad effect on Mr Phoenix too – that's why we need to get him to a hospital as soon as we can.'

'Nigel? Where is he?'

'In the staff room. But we have to find the parasite first, before it gets into anyone else.'

'Well, where is it now?'

'It's inside Dr Morrow – he's one of my colleagues at the centre. It jumped from Phoenix to him, then ... jumped through the window.'

'It did what?'

'It doesn't seem to care about the body it inhabits. It just uses it as a vehicle and a way of gaining information and knowledge.'

'But we don't know what it wants,' Sean added, 'though it seems it's after something specific – I think it'll keep attacking people until it finds it.'

Waites looked from Sean to James, waiting for one

of them to give him the slightest sign that it was all a big joke. No such luck. 'So this thing is outside somewhere?'

'Yeah, unless it's already got back in.'

'I don't much like the idea of going out there,' Waites said, turning to the window. 'But—' He stopped as he heard a bloodcurdling scream from above. 'What the hell was that?'

'I think it was Mrs Rees,' Sean said.

Confusion more than horror had gripped Mrs Rees initially, but now she had made some sort of sense of what her eyes were seeing. She was barely aware of Morrow standing very close behind her, almost breathing down her neck, as her eyes continued to dart all over the dreadful scene. It looked as though all the blood in Phoenix's body had evacuated itself, along with blobs of slushy matter – his liquefied organs. His face was a pallid death mask, pocked with sores and streaked with the blood that, in his final moments, had poured from his eyes – which were now staring, yellow and misshapen, while his mouth, agape, still oozed blood and matter.

Part of Emily Rees wanted to walk forward just to check that Phoenix was definitely dead; the other part of her wondered how she could be so stupid as to even entertain such a notion. Of course he was dead. And whatever had killed him could be highly infectious, possibly airborne. She could already have caught it, but touching him would surely be the most idiotic move imaginable. She was reminded of pictures she'd seen in biology textbooks of the effects of the Ebola virus. This was similar, though it couldn't be Ebola. Not here.

'Oh God,' came a voice over her shoulder. 'What a mess.'

She slowly turned to face Morrow, wondering as she did so what this strange man had to do with the appalling death of her colleague. As she looked into his eyes, she realized that this was not the same man she'd met earlier: something about him had changed drastically.

'You . . . you've got something to do with this. What's going on? What happened to Nigel?'

'Please,' Morrow implored, wiping blood and drool from his chin. 'Don't panic. I'm going to fix this somehow, but we have to make sure that no one leaves the school.' He moved towards her, his arms outstretched in an effort to placate.

'Keep away from me.' It was no longer his behaviour that frightened Emily Rees; it was the fact that he looked very ill, and could well be suffering from whatever had killed Nigel Phoenix. She didn't want him near her, much less touching her. She wanted to get as far away as possible.

'Just listen,' Morrow said, still moving forward. 'Please, just listen—'

But Emily Rees had heard enough: she turned and bolted out of the room and straight into the men's toilets. She went over to the smashed window, rain still blowing in, and looked out, down to the ground. It was too far to jump – she could break her legs. She heard Morrow approaching from the staff room, still offering words of comfort, so she entered one of the toilet cubicles and locked the door. Morrow shuffled in and stopped. She could hear his breathing.

'I'm sorry,' he said. 'I'm so sorry about all of this, but you have to listen. We are all in danger. We have to think of the children.'

'Please! Just get away from me.'

'I will, I will, I just . . .' There was a pause, then she heard him rush to the window and vomit out into the rain. It sounded rough, painful, like more than just the contents of his stomach were being brought up. He coughed, vomited again, then started to cry. She began to feel sympathy for him, but there was no way she was leaving this cubicle. No way on earth.

CHAPTER 15

Waites led the way, wondering what had happened to his quiet afternoon of marking papers. As if being caught in the mother of all storms wasn't bad enough, his world now seemed to have descended into *Invasion of the Bodysnatchers*. He still wasn't entirely sure what was going on, but the scream had sounded awful, so he led the way towards the staff room, once again hoping that this was all just one big wind-up.

Waites immediately saw the blood on the floor – lots of it – and then Phoenix's body; he was gagging at the appalling sight when Morrow staggered into the room, gasping for breath.

'It's in the system,' the doctor said, leaning against the wall as if he might collapse at any moment. Control of his body had been returned to him, but his limbs were now racked with pins and needles as sensation slowly returned.

'Mrs Rees is in there,' he said, pointing behind him. 'She's fine – she just locked herself in the cubicle when I ... I don't blame her. I must look awful.'

'I guess you must be Dr Morrow,' Waites said. 'What the hell happened?' He put his hand over his mouth at the smell that came from Phoenix's body.

'His body broke down,' Morrow replied, staring at the mess on the floor between them. 'I think the specimen carries an infection that remains even after it leaves its host. Now I've got it too.'

'What sort of infection?'

Until now Sean and his brother had been standing quietly in the doorway, still trying to take everything in. Morrow turned to look at them.

'James, did you tell Mr, er ...'

'Mr Waites. Dan,' Waites said.

'Did you tell Dan what it is we're up against?'

'Yes, I did. I think he might believe us now,' James replied.

'The specimen got into the water system. It could be anywhere.'

'Specimen?' Waites asked, perplexed. 'Just what exactly is it?'

'It's an unknown species with aggressive tendencies and is ... poisonous and apparently fatal if it infects you.'

'How do we kill it?'

'While it's in the pipe-work there's no way we can.

But if we do manage to get hold of it . . . I don't know.' Morrow shrugged his shoulders helplessly.

'What did it do to Nigel?'

'I think it secretes something that attacks the body of the host, making the organs turn to mush and bleed out.'

'Jesus, shouldn't we be phoning someone? Isn't there some government agency for dealing with this sort of thing?' Waites asked.

'Yes, but they wouldn't get here fast enough, especially in this weather.' Morrow's breathing was now growing laboured, and the colour had drained from his flesh. 'Do you understand what I've told you?'

'Yes, I think so.'

'Right, well, we need to think about possible strategies.'

'Strategies?'

'While it was in me I heard its thoughts, just as it could hear mine. If I concentrate I might be able to remember something that could help us stop it.' Morrow coughed painfully. 'It's more dangerous than you think . . . It used my body in ways I couldn't.'

'What do you mean?' Sean asked.

'The strength . . . it wasn't my own. It seems capable of doing things the body isn't used to, or isn't normally prepared to do. Sometimes we don't attempt things because we feel we haven't the strength, but usually it's our body telling us we might come to harm. When that thing was in me it was able to override those safety measures and do as it wished.'

'Like overclocking,' James said. The other three turned to him, confused. 'It's when you push your computer, or specifically the CPU, to operate at a higher speed than the manufacturer recommends in order to get more performance out of it. Risky, but most of the time effective if you know what you're doing – a bit like this creature.'

'Ha.' Morrow laughed, despite the situation. 'Yes ... Ignoring manufacturers' recommendations. Perhaps that accelerates the process of destruction set in motion when the creature enters a host.'

'Yeah,' James said, 'and when you push a computer too hard it either shuts itself down ... or burns out.'

Emily could hear voices from the direction of the staff room. No one was screaming, so perhaps things were under control. She stood up and moved closer to the door in an attempt to hear more. Suddenly there was a strange sound behind her, apparently coming from the wall. She waited and heard the sound again, lower down this time; it was like twisting metal. What was it? She forgot about the voices from the staff room temporarily and nearly jumped as the sound came from behind the toilet itself. Something was moving about in there, but what? She didn't want to open the door – but she didn't want to stay in the cubicle now either. Something was now splashing about in the toilet bowl, and she panicked, opening the door and inching away from the cubicle towards one of the hand basins. She stood there, still listening, still wondering what was going on.

The creature had already mapped the pipe-work of this part of the building in its memory. It could sense the woman's movement; could hear her breathing and could guess where she was now. Even as Emily Rees leaned against the basin in confused panic, the creature was working its way up around the system towards the tap; this time it moved soundlessly, its body squeezing smoothly along the pipes.

Emily stared at the cubicle door, waiting to see if anything emerged – unaware that something black and slimy was oozing out of the hot water tap behind her.

There was a splash, then another, and as Emily turned round to see what was going on, she was overcome by a feeling of dread. And then she saw it: a horrible, wriggling slug-like thing. She stared in disgust at it, then flinched as it coiled itself up and sprang towards her face. She stumbled backwards, slipped and fell to the floor, jarring her spine and banging her head against the cubicle partition. She blacked out.

Waites looked down at the floor, trying to process everything at once.

'This is too much. It just doesn't make any—'

'Please,' Morrow said. 'Is there a toilet I could use?'

'Yes, of course. Might be best to stay away from Mrs Rees if she's scared of you. You can use the boys' toilets downstairs.'

Waites ushered Morrow and the two brothers down the stairs. 'I'll go and check on Mrs Rees,' he told them. 'You boys wait here for me a second.' He turned and went back up the stairs.

'If I remember anything crucial I'll come and find you and Mr Waites,' Morrow said. 'I really need to be on my own right now though.'

'We understand,' Sean said. They watched him go into the toilet, wondering how long the poor man had left to live.

Waites almost bumped into Mrs Rees as she came out of the staff-room toilets.

'God, Emily, are you—?'

'Ah, er, Dan . . .'

'Come on, let's get you to the hall with the others.'

'Yes.'

'We have a crisis – it's best if you're not on your own right now.'

'Oh yes, of course. That doctor . . .'

'Yes, I'll explain it all, come on.' He ushered her through the staff room and down the steps. 'We all have to be very careful, Emily. There's a creature here in the school, something from the study centre. It's extremely dangerous. Nigel and Dr Morrow have already succumbed to its infection and we need to make sure it doesn't infect anyone else.'

As they all headed towards the main hall, Sean wondered what awful thing would happen next. The whole town could be submerged, judging by the sheer volume of water that had fallen on it, and if this bizarre parasite kept jumping from person to person, then dozens of people might be dead by morning. That's if they hadn't all drowned first.

It was as they passed the entrance doors that the full extent of the deluge became clear. Water from higher up the hill had been streaming down the road for some time, but now it had spread out and was coming into the school. Dark tendrils of water streaked across the floor like tentacles seeking something to grab hold of. They all stopped to watch in shock as the wide, slow-moving wave saturated the carpet and spread round the corner out of sight.

'Come on,' Waites said. 'Let's go.'

CHAPTER 16

'Headmaster,' said Mrs Rees as she spotted Mr Titus in the hall. 'Could I have a word please?'

'Of course.' From her expression it was clear that she needed to talk in private, so the headmaster took her off to the other side of the hall, away from the remaining pupils. 'What's wrong?'

'I didn't want to tell you this in front of the students because it's quite ... distressing, but ... Nigel is dead.'

Titus knew instantly that she wasn't joking: there was a horrible earnestness in her eyes. But there was clearly more bad news to come.

'I think it might have been something this odd doctor fellow did to him. He came in with a pupil and his brother earlier, behaving very oddly. All of a sudden, after speaking to this man, Nigel became very sick, and I'm worried that the doctor had something to do with it.'

'Good Lord. Where is this man now?'

'He's in the boys' toilets near the staff room. He looks extremely ill.'

'And what did you do with ... with Nigel?' The headmaster glanced around at the pupils, who were still chatting idly; he wondered how his day could possibly get any worse.

'He's still in the staff room but he's— Oh God, it's horrible!'

'We should call the police. Not that they'd be much good at the moment but ... we'd better call them anyway.' Titus went over to Waites and told him he would be in his office if there were any problems, then left with Mrs Rees.

As he closed his office door, he noticed that Mrs Rees had a rather strange expression on her face.

'Are you quite all right, Emily?'

'Yes, of course, headmaster,' she said as she moved closer.

James had been watching Mrs Rees since they'd left the staff room; now he decided to follow her to the headmaster's office to try and eavesdrop on their conversation. Something about her behaviour hadn't been quite right, and although he knew he was probably being paranoid, he had to have peace of mind. He approached the door of the office and put his ear to it. The voices were muffled, but he could tell that something was wrong. After a second or two he heard Titus's voice raised, then a shuffling and footsteps, then Mrs

Rees, more placating than panicked. He tried in vain to make out the words. Then he remembered that the office window looked out onto the grounds. If he went out into the rain he might be able to look in and see what was going on.

Retracing his steps, he went past the stairs and ducked outside through the double doors, straight into the unrelenting downpour. Almost immediately his clothes were drenched once more. He tried keeping to the side of the building, but there was no cover anywhere. Soon he was trudging through a water-logged flowerbed just outside the headmaster's office. He peeked carefully through the window, ready to whip his head back should the occupants turn round. At first all he could see was Mrs Rees's back, moving in a strange fashion; then, as more of the room was revealed, he realized that she was hugging the headmaster, a fierce, determined expression on her face. Mr Titus looked more confused than scared, wondering what on earth had come over her and trying to detach her without causing offence. Then, as James wondered what he should do – stay and watch or go and find the others – he saw something odd in the small washroom that was attached to the headmaster's office ...

The creature would have infected Emily Rees if she hadn't knocked herself out. But as it wriggled onto her body, it had decided that it needed someone stronger; someone who could help it find the answers it sought. It needed something – something it had been seeking for a long time – and it was sure the key to it was in this school somewhere . . . But where? It had slid away from the teacher's inert body and oozed up to the basin, squeezing itself back into the pipe. It had heard voices mention a headmaster. In Phoenix's mind it had come across this word too. It referred to someone in charge, in control. And from Phoenix it also knew the location of this individual's office.

James made up his mind: he ran back round into the building, then along to the headmaster's office. He burst in to find Mrs Rees crying on the shoulder of the headmaster, who was consoling her as best he could.

'James?' he asked when he saw the boy.

'It's in there . . . in the basin!' James pointed to the small washroom.

'What is?' the head asked, detaching himself from Mrs Rees.

'The thing! The specimen from the study centre!'

'The what?'

'It can't be,' Mrs Rees insisted. 'It's inside me. It attacked me. Oh God, what's going to happen to me?'

'But . . .' James was confused. 'But it can't be. You wouldn't be in control of yourself if it was.'

'But it was on me, in the staff toilets. I could feel it on my face before I passed out.'

'I saw it through the window,' James insisted. 'It's in there.'

'What's in there?' Titus asked, sounding like he was losing patience with the whole matter. He went into the washroom, switched on the light and looked around. 'Well?' he asked, turning back to James. 'There's nothing—'

At that moment it dropped from the skylight above them, partly because its target was in exactly the right spot but also because the light had startled it. It dropped onto Titus's face and slipped effortlessly into his mouth before he could do anything about it. He began thrashing about and making choking sounds, staring wide-eyed at the other two, imploring them for help.

Sean was wondering where James had got to and was about to ask Waites, when the teacher went over to talk to three remaining pupils, who were huddled around a mobile phone, reading a text message.

'Listen, guys, you'd better go home now,' he told them.

'But it's pouring, sir!' the boy said. 'We can't go out there.'

'Yeah. Besides, me and Steve live out of town,' said one of the two girls, 'and Emma's still waiting for her dad to get here. Mr Titus said we had to stay here because it wasn't safe to go outside.'

'Yes, well, we have a situation here now that means you'd be better off taking your chances outside. Is there a friend's house you can go to until you can get lifts home?'

'We could go to Stacey's – she lives in town and said we could go there if we couldn't get home.'

'Fine,' Waites said. 'Go to—'

His last words were cut off by a loud and horrifying scream. He quickly shared a knowing and anxious look with Sean, then turned back to the three startled pupils and said: 'Go! Now!'

'What the hell was that? What's—?'

'Just go,' Waites ordered.

They scooped up their bags and coats and headed for the exit, exchanging confused and frightened glances. Waites and Sean rushed out into the main hallway, then down the corridor towards where they thought the scream had come from. There was no one around, but Sean had the distinct feeling that something awful was very close by, possibly watching them at that moment. Then came a loud bang, like a heavy object being knocked over, and they turned in the direction of the headmaster's office.

Suddenly everything went quiet again. They looked at each other before proceeding, neither really knowing what to expect. Could James be in there with Mr Titus and Mrs Rees? Sean wondered. He didn't like to think what might have happened. As they approached the door, they heard what sounded like scratching on the other side, then saw the handle being twisted.

The door burst open and a very pale-looking Mrs Rees lurched towards them. They parted to avoid her, and watched in shock as she crashed into the window behind them. Neither Sean nor Mr Waites knew what to do; they just stared as she turned round, crying with fear and shaking her head in disbelief.

'It's in him now . . . Oh God.' Then she turned and ran down the corridor towards reception.

At first Sean and Waites were too stunned to move. They looked back at the office door, which was still ajar. Through the gap they could see only a sliver of window and the rain beating down outside.

'Come on,' Waites said. 'There's two of us. We can do this.'

'She said "him",' Sean muttered as though to himself. 'Did she mean Titus or . . . James . . . ? Where *is* he?'

'I don't know . . . But we have to stop this thing . . . somehow.' Waites carefully reached out and pushed the door open, trying not to make a sound. They could see papers, books and stationery strewn around; on the floor were shards of glass and a mound of dirt where a photograph frame had smashed and a plant had been knocked over. It was only when they were over the threshold that they caught sight of James standing over Titus's body in the far corner.

Oh no, Sean thought. *Please . . . No . . .*

CHAPTER 17

'We need to lock it up,' James said, still staring at the body slumped in the corner. He turned to look at Waites and his brother, who were still standing in the doorway. 'We need to do it while he's unconscious.'

Waites and Sean hesitated. The determined but scared look in James's eyes suggested he was still untouched, but how could they be certain? They approached him cautiously, and Waites helped him hoist Titus to his feet.

'Careful,' James whispered, as though worried the creature might hear. 'It might come back out at any second.'

'What happened?' Sean asked as they supported the unconscious headmaster by draping his arms around their shoulders.

'I was watching them from outside when I saw that ... thing coming out of the tap. I ran in here to stop it but ... I was too late. Once it was inside him, I pushed him and he fell against the wall, banging his head. I don't know if he'll be out for long, but we need to get him locked away before he – or rather it – wakes up.'

They dragged the headmaster out of the office and into the corridor, past the windows overlooking the school playing fields. Sean groaned inwardly. The rain seemed to be coming down even harder than before. How was that possible? How could there be so much water in the sky? It looked like night out there too, even though the sun wasn't anywhere near setting yet.

'Where are we going to put him?' Sean asked.

'How about the cupboard in the chemistry lab?' James suggested. 'We can lock him in there.'

'Yes, but there's too much dangerous stuff around,' Waites said. 'And there's a window too. He might escape. I know, we'll put him in that cupboard in the hall where the chairs are kept. It's secure and there are no windows.'

They turned and carried the headmaster back towards the hall; his feet banged against the steps leading down. When they had crossed the hall, Waites tutted angrily, realizing he'd done something stupid.

'We haven't got the key,' he said.

'I know where it is,' Sean said. 'The caretaker keeps it in a mug on his desk. I saw him get it out when I had to help him set up for assembly once. He doesn't keep it in the locked cabinet with the others because he uses it so often. I'll go and get it.'

'OK. But hurry up. I don't like to think what might happen when our friend here wakes up.'

Sean nodded, turned and ran out of the hall, then up a small flight of stairs to the caretaker's office.

Emily Rees was beyond distraught. She'd already seen what had happened to Nigel Phoenix, and could only assume that the same was going to happen to her. She couldn't stop crying, and her thoughts, rather than dwelling on her inevitable fate, were now centred on her husband and children. Mark would still be at work, but her children would be at home, probably watching television or doing their homework. She realized she wasn't going to see them again, and the thought horrified her.

She suddenly heard a deep, painful coughing from the boys' toilets. She had a good idea who it was, and wanted to keep as far away as possible, yet she had a powerful urge to know what to expect, so she went in. She saw him straight away, slumped against the far wall; his hands lay in his lap, covered in blood. He looked up at her, his face pale, pitiful. She approached carefully, unsure of what he might do in his condition.

'Are you OK?' he asked.

'No,' Emily replied, cringing at the sight of his sunken, bloodshot eyes. 'I . . . What's happening to me? It was inside my head.'

'Probably the same thing that's happening to me. The same that happened to Nigel. I'm sorry,' he said, looking away.

Emily stood there staring at him, eyes imploring, waiting for some words of hope.

'It's best you stay here,' Morrow told her. 'Just in case whatever's happening to your body is infectious. I don't think it's airborne; I think it's something only the specimen can put in your system, but I could be wrong. It could be highly contagious, so we need to remain here until the authorities arrives. Besides . . . do you really want your family to see what's going to happen to you?' It was callous but it had to be said. He coughed and spat a wad of red mucus onto the floor.

Mrs Rees gazed at him in horror, her stomach turning. 'I . . . I can't. I'm sorry.' She started to back away. 'I have to see them. I have to see my children before . . . You understand?'

'No!' he shouted, leaning forward with one hand outstretched, before arching his back in a spasm of pain. He groaned as the agony consumed him. 'For God's sake,' he cried, his eyes closed at the agonizing sensation in his spine. 'You can't leave! You can't leave, do you hear me? You could have a disease inside you! You could end up killing everyone!'

But Emily Rees was gone.

CHAPTER 18

The key was lying at the bottom of the large green mug on the caretaker's desk, exactly where Sean had expected it to be. As he picked it up, he was aware of movement outside the window. He turned to see the drenched figure of Mrs Rees, stumbling and then falling, splashing on the sodden ground. He watched, his mouth open, as she ran on behind the annexe towards the main road that led to the town.

Why is she running? Sean wondered. He hurried back to the hall and found the other two waiting anxiously by the cupboard door with the inert body of the headmaster.

'I just saw Mrs Rees,' he said, handing the key to Waites. 'She was running away from the school. I'm going to check on Dr Morrow, see if he knows anything about it. I think something might be wrong. She wouldn't just take off like that.'

'All right,' Waites said. 'But hurry back. James and I will get Titus into the cupboard.'

It didn't take Sean long to return to the toilets and find out from Morrow that Mrs Rees believed she was infected.

'You have to find her,' Morrow implored. 'She mustn't spread the infection.'

'OK, I'll try.' Sean headed back to the main hall, wondering how he had been given so much responsibility. After all, was he really capable of doing anything to stop it?

He thought about Mrs Rees and the effect the disease would have on her and her family. If she was indeed infected and died in the middle of town, amidst thousands of other people, they would be facing a far greater disaster than the one they were currently trying to deal with. The authorities would then determine the source of the problem and descend on the school before he, James and Waites were able to deal with the parasite. Right now they were the only ones with any understanding of it. The government would have to quarantine the place. The creature had to be destroyed before it got away.

'We have to stop her,' Sean said simply when he'd explained the situation to the others.

'All right,' Waites said. 'You and James go after her and bring her back here – by force if necessary. I'll stay and watch Titus.'

'Maybe you should go and see Morrow before he ... you know,' Sean suggested. 'Just in case he's remembered something that could help us kill this creature – he said he would try to think back in case there was something . . .'

'Maybe I will. But I don't think I should leave that thing unguarded for long.'

'Yes, do be careful, Mr Waites,' James said. 'If that thing manages to get out . . .'

'All right. You two, just go. Go and find Emily before it's too late.'

Sean led his brother out of the hall, pushing the entrance doors open and grimacing at the ferocity of the rain. He pulled the zip on his coat up as far as it would go and tugged the already wet hood over his head. But suddenly he realized James was no longer behind him; he was standing by the stairs, deep in thought.

Sean shook his head and opened the door again. 'Come on, James, we have to find her!'

His brother looked up, confused at first, then nodded and followed him. 'Sorry, I just remembered something . . .'

'What?'

'Oh, nothing . . . Let's go.'

They ran across the car park towards the main road. They had considered taking James's car, but the roads could now be so flooded that it would only be a hindrance. It was even darker now; the sky was covered in thick, heavy clouds. They crossed to the narrow pavement and ran down the winding hill towards the town, hoping Mrs Rees hadn't found somewhere to hide.

Waites was pacing up and down outside the cupboard, biting his nails and wondering what he would do once the thing woke up and started trying to get out. He had no idea whether the cupboard would hold it – or whether he could overpower the possessed headmaster if he got free. There was no sound from within, so there was no need to panic just yet, but the time would inevitably come. And he couldn't help wondering how long Morrow had left. Had the man remembered something useful – something that could be used to kill this creature and reverse the effects of the infection? If the man had information, it might be valuable. Perhaps he should risk leaving the headmaster unattended for a short while and go and talk to Morrow before it was too late. He paced a while longer, his eyes on the locked door, then made up his mind: he ran across the hall, then out into the corridor.

Morrow had coughed up so much blood he couldn't believe there was any left. Surely he didn't have much time now. The pain within had been replaced by a numbness that made him feel shrunken and deflated. His head felt like a huge hand was squeezing it, and his teeth were loose, and moved every time his dry tongue passed over them. He didn't feel human any more; he felt like a different creature altogether. With his remaining energy, he prayed that Waites or the boys would come back so he could pass on the piece of information he had just remembered – otherwise they'd have no chance of beating the thing.

He waited, his laboured breathing the only thing disturbing the silence. His head was hurting so much now that even thinking was painful. *Please*, he willed. *Please come*. But it sounded as if everyone had gone – he had been abandoned. *Such a big tomb*, he thought wryly. Then, without warning, there was a huge explosion in his chest, and all at once the veins in his arms felt like they had been pulled tight, constricted. *Oh hell*, he thought. *Here it comes*. And unlike Emily Rees, what was on his mind as death came sweeping towards him was not his family, but the overwhelming need to deliver his message.

By the time Waites reached the boys' toilets, Morrow was dead. He'd actually begun speaking to him and only stopped when he saw the glazed look in the man's staring, lifeless eyes. His shoulders sagged. He was too late. But as he approached the blood-soaked corpse he saw what Morrow had done with his last few seconds of life. A message was written in the man's own blood on the tiled floor nearby.

Sall . . .

Morrow's finger lay curled near the last letter, its job apparently done. But the message couldn't be complete. *Sall* . . . What did it mean? Perhaps Morrow had been trying to write *Sally*. If so, who was she, and what was her involvement in all this? Waites knelt and looked again into the dead man's eyes.

'What were you trying to say?'

He remained there a moment longer, then remembered his captive in the hall. He was tempting fate by staying away any longer than he needed to. If that thing got out and headed towards town, it would be all over. He left the toilets, jogging back towards the hall and hoping the headmaster was still unconscious.

CHAPTER 19

Emily Rees reached a very important decision as she staggered down towards the high street in the rain. She could go home, collapse into her family's arms, tell them she loved them, then die in front of them in a horrific manner, or she could get as far away as she could and die somewhere no one would find her. Her family would still be traumatized, but at least they would never see her final, appalling moments; they would not be left with that awful memory.

She reached the bottom of the hill and saw cars everywhere, some parked on the pavement, others backed up all the way along the high street. Their owners had obviously abandoned them and sought refuge elsewhere. About halfway down there appeared to have been a collision, but there were no emergency vehicles present: no doubt they were more urgently needed elsewhere. The torrent surged through the jam of vehicles and Emily didn't like the idea of climbing over them, only to slip and injure herself. Looking to her right, she saw a path that led away from the town. It meant crossing a stream that would inevitably be flooded, but it might still be safer. She turned and jogged along it, sending up cascades of muddy water with every step.

As she ran she fantasized about heading home instead, seeing the lights on, someone moving about inside. If she got close enough to the house she might be able to hear the television, maybe even her kids ... She shook her head. No, she mustn't allow herself to succumb to the temptation. She shrugged the thoughts away and continued along the path that led to the swollen brook. When she reached it her heart sank. It was almost twice its normal size and the stepping stones that normally allowed access from one bank to the other were now completely submerged. She stared at the raging water and shook her head. This was as far as she could go.

Behind her, somewhere in the town, she heard a loud splash – she didn't know it, but it was the sound of the small public toilet block collapsing into the river. She gazed deep into the swirling torrent. She wasn't ready to die. Not yet. She backed away from the water and found a spot by a tree where she could sit and watch the patterns in the dark, angry brook.

She remained there, for an eternity it seemed, waiting for the pain to start, then for the end to come ...

* * *

Waites was relieved to find the door to the cupboard still closed. He pressed an ear to one of the doors. He could hear nothing to begin with, but just as he was about to move away . . . a hoarse, tired voice:

'Is that you, Daniel?'

Waites froze. It was certainly Titus, although he sounded strained and in pain. Knowing that something foreign could be inside the headmaster, controlling him, Waites found the words chilling. He didn't answer, but kept his ear to the door, curious to hear what the thing said next. The four words were repeated, then there was a cough followed by movement. Whether this was the creature trying to make itself more comfortable or to find a possible means of escape, he couldn't be sure, but it seemed to be having difficulty. He sat down and kept his ear to the crack in the door, wondering what the creature was prepared to say or do to secure its freedom. He heard grunting and panting, and what sounded like another exclamation of pain.

'Whoever is out there' – the voice returned, clearer now than before, and more authoritative – 'would you kindly tell me what on earth is going on? What am I doing in here?' Waites remained silent. 'Hello?' The voice was angrier, more impatient now – Titus was in his element, Waites thought. There was a pause, then the headmaster started banging on the door in frustration.

'I'm not unlocking the door,' Waites said firmly.

The banging stopped. 'What?'

'I said I'm not unlocking this door.'

'Do you mind telling me why, Daniel?'

'You know why.'

'I'm afraid I don't.'

'Yes, you do,' Waites replied, shaking his head. 'This is crazy,' he muttered to himself. He hadn't been trained to deal with alien parasites, or whatever this thing was. Unruly pupils were bad enough, but this thing was a killer.

'Look,' the headmaster began, 'if this is something to do with Emily . . . I'm not sure what happened. She attacked me. I tried to throw her off and then . . . I don't know what happened. I must have hit my head.'

'What do you want?' Waites asked, ignoring the explanation.

'What do you mean?'

'What was worth killing them for?'

'Killing who? Are you daft?'

'This is pointless.' It was. It was useless trying to get anything out of this thing. It clearly wasn't stupid: like any prisoner it would deny everything until it had an opportunity to get away.

'My head really hurts, Daniel. I think it's bleeding.'

Waites didn't respond. This new tack was to be expected. It was trying to get sympathy now, appealing to his sense of humanity, his compassion. It would no doubt exaggerate its pain and misery until it got the result it wanted. Except that moment would not come. Waites wasn't going to give in and allow the creature to kill again.

'Did you hear what I said, Daniel?' The voice was almost pathetic, most unlike the headmaster's normal manner. It was just the two of them in the school now. With the rain refusing to let up and the emergency services no doubt already stretched to the limit, it was likely to stay 'just the two of them' for quite some time. *Oh God*, Waites thought. *This is going to be a long night*.

'She could be anywhere,' James said, spitting out rainwater.

'I know, but . . .' Already Sean could see the futility of trying to track down the teacher. Who knew where she had gone? He heard people shouting and turned to see three men wading through the water, which had now completely swamped the road where the first few shops began. They seemed to be enjoying themselves. Sean turned back to James to see a look of deep concentration on his face.

'What is it?'

'Oh, I was just thinking . . . Maybe we should go back to the study centre.'

'What? The road there was bad enough earlier on; it'll be worse now.'

'I know, but if there's a way of stopping that thing, the answer might be there.'

'But it's locked up in that cupboard now. As long as it stays there until we can get help, we should be all right.'

'Yeah, but help is a long way off. Look at all the water. It'll take ages to sort things out. The town flooded before, remember? It took a while to recover from that, and this is worse.'

'Well, maybe we should just go back up to the school then. Make sure Mr Waites is OK before we do anything else.'

'Yeah, all right.'

'Better phone Mum and Dad again too,' Sean said. 'They'll be worried.'

'What was the black thing?' Titus asked after another long pause.

'What black thing?' Waites responded non-committally.

'The thing that came out of the tap. I . . . I saw it. Like a big slug or something.'

'That'll be you,' Waites told him.

'Me?'

'The "big slug". That's you.'

'Have . . . have you lost your mind?'

'You got into Titus's head and now you're controlling him.'

'That's ridiculous, Dan.'

'Is it? You did the same thing to Nigel and that doctor – who is now dead too, incidentally. You certainly made a mess of him.'

'That thing is not inside me! The last I saw of it, it was crawling into James's mouth.'

Waites didn't reply. This could so easily be an attempt to confuse him or plant doubt in his mind. If he were the creature, wouldn't he do the same thing? And yet the possibility couldn't be completely discounted. He and Sean had reached the headmaster's office after the switch had occurred. Emily had said it was 'in him' – which could have meant either Titus or James. Waites felt more and more unnerved as he began to realize the implications of his discovery.

'What is it, Daniel? What is that thing?' Titus asked, sounding tired, confused and frightened. 'It looked hideous and . . . it seemed to have a mind of its own.'

Waites said nothing; he was trying to think.

'Look, Dan, whatever's been going on here, I swear to you, that thing is not inside me.'

'I'm not listening,' Waites insisted.

But he was. Of course he was.

CHAPTER 20

The two brothers ducked down to shelter under a tree and phoned their parents. Rather than waste time trying to explain the unexplainable, they just told them they were waiting at the school for the weather to improve with some other pupils and teachers, which was partially true. Mum was livid that Sean still wasn't home, but nothing could be done about that. When James hung up, they started back up the hill towards the school, wondering what they'd find when they got there. Sean was already imagining horrible scenarios, most of them centred around the creature escaping and disappearing into the night. At the top of the hill they could see water gushing down the road like a river.

Sean shouted at his brother: 'James! Are you serious about the study centre?'

His brother didn't reply – he evidently hadn't heard; instead he just crossed the road and jogged into the school car park.

'Because we'll never get there in the car now,' Sean went on.

'Come on,' James said, waiting for him to catch up. 'Let's see how Waites is getting on.'

They splashed through the reception area and headed for the main hall. Waites was pacing again now. He looked up and saw them standing in the doorway.

'Sean, are you OK?' he asked.

'Yeah, we're fine.' Sean hurried over to the teacher. 'We couldn't find Mrs Rees though – she could be any-where by now.'

'Then it's out of our hands. We'll just have to hope that no one else has found her. Sean, can I have a quick word?'

Both Sean and his brother found the request odd, but neither said anything. Sean walked away with Waites so that they were out of earshot, leaving James by the cupboard.

'Sean, I know what you're going to say, but before we decide what to do next, we have to consider the possibility that . . .' Waites hesitated while he found the right words.

'What?' Sean followed Waites's gaze as it rested momentarily on James.

'The possibility that James might have been infected by that thing and not Titus.'

'What? But he hasn't been! You know that.'

'Shh! Keep your voice down. I know that's how it seems, but we could be wrong. Look, if it is in Titus it could well have been trying to convince me that James is infected so I'll set it free – I'm aware of that, but still . . . there is a chance. Emily said it was in "him". She didn't say which "him".'

Sean looked again at his brother, unwilling to believe that he could be the monster now. That couldn't be true. The ramifications were too horrible to consider.

'No,' he said firmly. 'If it was in him I'd know by now. It would have done something or said something to give itself away. It would . . .' He winced and started rubbing his forehead.

'Are you OK?'

'Yeah. I just . . . It's from the other day, I think. The run. Still not fully recovered.'

'Here, sit down on the end of the stage.'

Sean did as instructed, perching on the edge. As he looked around, he realized that the hall itself, and indeed the rest of the school, seemed strange now, tainted by the bizarre, the horrific.

'Look, I know my own brother,' Sean said. 'He can't be infected, and besides, while we were out he had plenty of opportunities to either attack me or escape. And why would that thing want to come back here?'

'I don't know. Did he say anything to you that sounded odd, or out of character?'

'No, I don't think so.'

'OK, well, look, just be careful. We can't be certain of anything right now, so let's just be on our guard. You stay here a sec. I'll go and see how Titus is.'

'What about Dr Morrow?' Sean asked, suddenly remembering the dying man.

'He's . . . He didn't make it, I'm afraid.'

'Oh.' Sean looked down at his feet as they swung idly below him. He glanced over at his brother, again praying that the thing hadn't got to him. To have to watch something so horrible happen to someone he loved was unthinkable.

'He tried to leave us a message though,' Waites said. 'He wrote it on the floor.'

'What did it say?'

'Sall.'

'Sall? As in Sally?'

'I don't know. Maybe. Do you know anyone called Sally that might have something to do with this?'

'No.'

'What about James?'

'Well, he worked at the study centre with Dr Morrow – maybe it's someone they both know.'

'Let's ask him.'

Meanwhile James had heard the odd word from Sean and Waites's conversation, but had been unable to make out the gist of what they were saying. He'd seen them look at him though, and had guessed what they might be discussing. Not good.

He inched towards the cupboard. He thought he could hear breathing inside, but he might have imagined it. And then the man inside spoke.

'Who's there? Is that you, Daniel?'

James didn't reply, but instead turned his back and leaned against the door.

The voice came again. 'Look, please let me out now. This is ridiculous. I told you – that thing, whatever it is, went inside that boy – Sean's brother. It's not in me, for Christ's sake! Get me out of here.'

James considered this while the voice continued, 'It's you, isn't it, boy?' it said all of a sudden. 'I know it's you. It's inside you. You do know that, don't you? You might not remember, but I saw. I saw it! And now it's me that's locked up instead of you!'

James peered through the crack in the door, fancying that two eyes were staring out accusingly. 'Shut up,' he said coldly. 'You don't know what you're talking about.'

'James?'

'Yeah?' James turned round, looking startled.

'Are you OK?' Sean asked.

'Don't listen to him,' Waites said, meaning the man in the cupboard. 'He'll try anything to get out.'

'Oh yeah, I know. I just—'

'Dr Morrow's dead,' Sean said.

'Oh God.'

'Yeah, I know . . . but he left us a message: "Sall". We think he might have been trying to tell us something.'

'Sall?'

'He may not have been able to finish the message,' Waites said, testing the cupboard door to make sure it was still secure, 'but we think he may have meant to write "Sally". Do you know of anyone at the study centre called Sally?'

James thought for a second. 'Yeah, there is! One of the marine specialists, Sally Cooper. She's only there on Saturdays and Wednesday evenings, but she knows . . . knew Dr Morrow quite well. She shared an office with one of the other scientists. Maybe there's something there that can help us. I was thinking we should go there anyway. That's where the thing came from. If there's nothing in Sally's office that can help, then maybe Dr Morrow wrote something in his notes.'

'Maybe,' Waites said. 'But "Sall" could mean anything. I think we should stay here and wait for the rain to stop. In the meantime we can decide what to do with that thing.'

'But it will probably have killed Titus by then,' James said. 'If it leaves him, it can probably get out of the cupboard somehow. I'm sure the answer is at the research centre.'

'You seem awfully keen to go back there,' Waites said. Sean could sense his suspicion – a suspicion he now found himself sharing.

'I just ... I just think we should do everything we can to end this. What if it keeps raining until morning? We don't want to be stuck here all night with that thing.'

They were all silent for a few moments. Waites was clearly thinking things over.

'All right,' he said at length. 'We'll go, but we can't leave him here.' They all eyed the cupboard. 'We can't be sure that cupboard will contain him. If it leaves Titus, it could go anywhere. We'll have to take him with us.'

CHAPTER 21

The bridge was now all but submerged. The raging waters thundered through and against it relentlessly. Cracks had already appeared along its length and some stonework had long since washed away. The bridge's architects had not made provision for a flood of this magnitude all those decades ago. The car park of the nearby pub was completely swamped; the fields on the other side were now a vast lake. It was like the end of the world. The pub owners were staring at the waters swirling around the ground-floor bar, wading around in their wellington boots and wondering if there was actually anything they could do. But once the sewage-tainted water was in, that was it.

The path that ran along the river towards the park was no longer visible. Nearby, the supermarket was flooded with over a foot of water. Packets of noodles, crisps and other light debris floated lazily around in the muddy, smelly water, as the shop's manager swore and went on trying to get his superior on the phone. His staff were waiting to be told what to do, some of them wishing they'd gone home when their shift finished instead of agreeing to stay and help.

The water stretched all the way up the high street. Had it been clean water, the damage would have been bad enough, but now there was sewage to contend with.

Along Market Street people were wading around the site where the public toilets had stood. Most of the small brick building had fallen into the swollen brook below it, along with a large section of wall and brick paving. Rubble marked its original location, like an open, jagged wound. The town's drainage system was no longer functioning. Blockages that hadn't been dealt with had pushed water back up out of the drains, so there was nowhere for it to escape.

Orchard Wells was already struggling with one catastrophe. It didn't need another.

'He'll just attack us! Why can't we leave him here?' Sean was panicking now. He wanted the creature to stay locked up, and didn't see why they had to take him along with them.

'We can't do both things,' Waites said, trying to remain calm. 'We should stay together. Getting to the study centre will be dangerous. We can't leave him here – like I said, the thing might leave him and we know it can get around – we won't know where it's gone. This way, we can keep an eye on it at least.'

'But how are we going to tie him up?' James asked. 'Morrow survived that fall from the window when he was possessed. He told us that thing gave him abnormal strength, remember? I don't think we're going to be able to restrain it.'

There was a moment of silence as Waites considered this.

'Well, we've got to tie him up somehow.'

'Ha, good luck. If that's your plan, you're on your own.'

'If he tries anything we'll have to subdue him.'

'Yeah,' Sean said. 'That thing is really sensitive to blows on the head, isn't it? If we hit Titus hard it should knock him out.'

'I hope you're right,' Waites said doubtfully. 'We should also cover our mouths to stop that thing getting in.'

'That ... won't be necessary,' came the voice in the cupboard. 'There's nothing wrong with me. And if you're willing to let me out to prove that, I can promise you there'll be no funny business.'

Waites looked at the two brothers. 'Why should we believe you?'

'Oh, come on, Daniel, for God's sake ...' They could hear the headmaster's laboured breathing now. He was standing right by the crack in the door. 'It's me! Just open the door ... I promise ... I promise I won't do anything. I'll go with you wherever you want. Besides, pretty soon it'll become quite obvious to all of us where the monster really is.'

At this, Sean couldn't help glancing over at his brother, who in turn understood the meaning of it.

'It's not in *me!*' James blurted out defensively. 'It's in *him*, I saw it. He's just trying to—'

'Calm down,' Waites said. 'It's OK. For now let's just . . . Mr Titus, we're going to let you out. But I'm telling you now, if you try anything, we're going to have to use force.'

'Oh, this is ridiculous . . .' came the reply. 'How on earth did all this happen?' There was a shuffling and a coughing from within. 'Just please let me out – I'm in no state to do anything. This is just so stupid . . .'

Sean looked at his brother again. James looked uncomfortable. They were all scared and apprehensive, but James also looked like he was hiding something.

'Right, you two,' Waites said. 'I'm going to open the door slowly. When I unlock it, cover your mouths and be ready to run if he tries anything. I'll tackle him myself if it all goes wrong – just get yourselves away from here. Right?'

'What are you saying? We're not going to leave if he attacks you,' Sean said.

'Yeah,' James agreed. 'We're all in this together. We all tackle him if we need to.'

'I just don't want you guys getting . . . you know.'

'Yeah, I know,' James said. 'But still, we're not leaving you alone with him.'

'All right then. Ready? Hang on . . .' Waites covered his mouth with one hand, wondering what it would be like to have that crazy, wriggling monstrosity trying to burrow its way up into his brain. 'Nah, this is no good. Sean, does Mr Cole keep the fencing equipment in that cupboard?'

'No, it's in the store cupboard in his office – why?'

'Go and get three face guards.'

Sean made his way to Mr Cole's office. It was unlocked and, luckily, so was the store cupboard. He rummaged around, spilling most of the contents onto the floor until he found three mesh face guards, which he took back to the others. He handed one to Waites, then the other, nervously, to his brother, who noticed something was wrong.

'What is it?' James asked.

'What? Nothing.'

'I'm OK, really.'

'I know.' Sean went and stood next to Waites.

The teacher put on the face guard, then inserted the key into the lock of the cupboard. He glanced back to make sure the two boys had protected their faces, then turned the key.

The sound was somehow louder than it should have been. It seemed to echo and linger, as though heralding some awful event. There was a final click, then Waites turned the handle and slowly opened the door.

The interior was in darkness, but they could see piled

chairs, gym equipment and a projector screen. However, the headmaster was nowhere to be seen. The cupboard extended to the left and right of the door: he must be hiding somewhere out of sight, but why? Was the sudden light blinding him, or had he panicked and decided he'd rather stay there after all?

Waites was peering around nervously. 'Titus? Mr Titus, where are you?'

There was silence for several seconds; then the headmaster burst screaming out of the darkness: his arms were outstretched, bleeding, swollen, covered in weeping sores and welts, and from his mouth protruded the end of a writhing black slug like an ebony tongue.

Sean was so shocked he staggered backwards and fell. James turned and ran towards the windows overlooking the playing fields, and it was only Waites's quick reactions that prevented him from being cornered by the headmaster. The teacher dived for Titus's legs, bringing him crashing to the floor; he banged his head hard and lost consciousness again.

James was about to bring a boot down hard on the tail end of the slug, but it quickly pulled itself back inside the headmaster's mouth.

James swore and scowled at the unconscious headmaster, annoyed that the opportunity to destroy their enemy had been lost. 'So what now?'

CHAPTER 22

'We'll carry him to my car,' Waites said, getting to his feet. 'Come on. You guys grab an arm each. I'll take his legs.'

Sean and James took hold of the man's arms gingerly, watching his mouth in case the creature decided to make another break for freedom. They turned him over and lifted him, surprised by how heavy he was. Sean watched him carefully as they carried him towards the steps: his head was lolling to one side, his mouth open. Was that a gasp? There were also red, bleeding sores on the back of Titus's neck. Sean wondered what the creature was planning to do at that moment. Would it stay inside the headmaster until it saw a chance to escape, or was it intending to wait until it had one of them alone before emerging and attacking? Either way, Sean didn't want to be alone with it. As they negotiated the steps, he nearly lost hold of Titus's arm, and glanced at Waites. However, all the teacher's attention was focused on Titus's mouth.

'Right, guys, careful now. I'll try and open the door. Turn him round ... God, I can hardly see through this thing. Hang on, put him down a second. I've got a better idea.'

He took off the face guard and put it on Titus, securing it as tightly as he could. Sean and James removed their face guards too.

'Right, that should stop it from getting out. We'll tie him up properly at the centre. Come on.'

They picked up the body again and slowly turned so that Waites could shoulder the door open. As they passed through, the doors banged twice against the head-master's body. They carried him through the hallway and out into the car park. The rain seemed to have eased slightly, but the path was covered in water, and when James accidentally stepped onto the grass, it was like stepping into a bog.

'My car's on the far side,' Waites said.

'That figures,' James said, already showing signs of tiring.

They splashed across the car park until Waites told them to stop.

'Right, just put him down gently while I get the car open,' he said.

They laid him down in the water; his face was paler now, almost luminous in the dark, but with more sores visible on his forehead and cheeks. Waites took out his car keys and unlocked his old Vauxhall Corsa, opening a back door so that they could manhandle the headmaster inside.

'One of you will have to sit back here with him,' Waites said.

Sean and James both stared at him, horrified, neither one willing to volunteer.

'Come on, we don't have time—'

'All right,' James said. 'I will.'

'No, I will,' Sean countered.

'I'll do it,' James insisted firmly.

'No!' Sean was adamant now, his fear gone, his desire to protect his brother stronger.

'James,' Waites said, handing over the car keys, 'you drive. I'll sit in the back with our friend here.'

The brothers didn't argue. They lifted, pulled and shoved the headmaster into the vehicle, trying to manoeuvre him into something resembling a sitting position, then got in themselves; Waites was as close to his door and as far from the unconscious man as possible. He knew that thing was still alive and kicking inside the man's body, and he was already panicking at the idea of what would happen if it managed to 'jump ship' again.

James started the engine, flicking the front and rear windscreen wipers on. Sean buckled up his seat belt and looked in the rear-view mirror. He could only see

Waites's profile, but it was enough to tell that he was very anxious and uncomfortable. Titus's head was lolling back on the seat, his mouth wide open behind the mesh of the face guard. Sean imagined the black slug shooting out and oozing through the mesh, shredding itself then somehow miraculously re-forming and darting towards the back of his head. How much contact with the thing did you need before it killed you? he wondered. Did you merely have to touch it, or did it have to be inside you? And how long before it was able to regain control of the headmaster's body? If it did so while they were in the car it could be disastrous. As James reversed the car out of its space, Sean tried not to dwell on such things.

The car sent wave after wave of water across the car park as they moved towards the road. Unsurprisingly there were no other vehicles: everyone was either at home or waiting out the weather somewhere or helping others get out of harm's way. This time James took the back road to the study centre, hoping that the water wouldn't be too high.

'So what do you know of this Sally?' Waites asked, trying to take his mind off his fellow passenger. 'What did you say she did at the centre?'

'Well, I'm not really sure,' James said, peering ahead into the rain and darkness. 'I know she helped Dr Morrow quite a bit so she must be into marine life, but she kept snakes and things too. Perhaps we'll find out when we get there.'

'Well, whatever it was they were doing, Morrow used his last few moments on this earth to point us to it. Hopefully we can rid ourselves of this . . . thing before it does any more damage. Jesus . . . how the hell are we going to explain the mess at the school?'

Neither James nor Sean could think of a reply.

'I don't know,' Sean said after a while. 'But they'll realize it was an infection of some kind. I mean, it doesn't exactly look like murder.'

'No.' Waites looked out of the window, wishing it was light again, but knowing there were many hours of darkness still to come.

'God, it feels like this is the end, you know? Everything's happening at once,' James said as he slowed down for a bend in the road. It was unlikely there would be other traffic around, but he wasn't taking any chances. The rain blocked out any other sound, and as the car made its way along the waterlogged country lanes, the occupants could almost imagine they were alone in the world.

'Nearly there now,' James said, turning to Sean after what felt like an eternity.

Sean was peering out at the road ahead too – what he could see of it at least. He hadn't looked behind for a couple of minutes now, but when he happened to glance in the mirror again, what he saw made him cry out.

The headmaster's body was still sitting slumped, his head lolling backwards and moving slowly from side to side, but his eyes were now open.

Sean's cry caused James to lose concentration for a second, the car swerving across the road. 'What is it?' he asked, still straining to see the road ahead.

'He's awake!' Sean said, eyes glued to the mirror as Titus slowly lifted his head.

'Oh, shit,' Waites said. 'Move it, James!'

'We're nearly there, just round—'

But it was too late. With an unearthly groan, Titus raised his hands towards Waites's neck. The teacher was surprised by the headmaster's unnatural strength. The man was panting in his face now, and Waites expected to see something wriggle from his mouth and try to fight its way through the face guard.

'Here it is,' James shouted desperately. He swerved off the main road a little faster than he should have and started down the winding drive towards the lake and the study centre. The car rose and dipped over the bumps and potholes, throwing the occupants around.

'Oh God,' Sean heard Waites mutter behind him. 'I can see it.'

Waites started screaming and struggling with Titus, desperately trying to keep their mouths apart to stop the creature from switching host. James was also panicking, glancing in the mirror, then looking over his shoulder. It was Sean who noticed first that the car was moving dangerously close to the edge of the road, which was raised above the fields on either side. Sean cried out as James turned the wheel hard to the right, but it was too late.

The vehicle left the road, veered onto its side, the wheels churning the mud and sending it flying up behind them, then flipped over, rolling twice before settling back on its wheels with a loud, metallic moan.

CHAPTER 23

Sean's head was pounding. He'd half expected to pass out – that was what people did when they were in a car accident, but apart from being thrown about and bruising his shoulder, he was fine. But his head was pounding from the whiplash. It was like he'd been standing next to a loudspeaker on maximum volume for an hour. He felt like crying, the pain was so bad. He turned to his brother, who was just sitting there, his hands back on the wheel, staring through the windscreen in shock.

'Are you OK?' he asked.

'Yeah, I think so. Must have hit my head on some-thing though. I feel all right . . . Jesus, this car must have been made before airbags were invented. We were lucky.'

A back door opened and Sean heard Waites scrambling out. He and James got out too and the three of them congregated behind the vehicle. The car was a wreck. Three windows had shattered, one rear wheel had been crushed by the weight of the chassis, a headlight was missing, parts of the frame had buckled and there was a large dent in the roof. The one functioning headlight illuminated the area around them, though the interior of the vehicle was still in darkness. Sean thought he could see Titus, sitting bolt upright again, facing straight ahead. He looked at Waites.

'Did it . . . ?'

'What? Get me? No, of course not.' Waites wiped water from his face and spat, not taking his eyes off the car.

James glanced at him uncertainly.

'What? I'm telling you, it didn't get me. Look, the face guard is still on, you can see.'

'So what do we do now?' James asked, still testing his limbs to see if anything had been injured.

'We need to get him into the centre. How far is it?'

'It's just down there,' James said, pointing along the road.

'OK then. I'll have to knock him out. We'll drag him . . . Once we get him inside—'

He was interrupted by the sound of a car door opening. Sean wasn't sure how much of the water in his eyes was rain and how much was tears from the pain, but through it all he could just make out the door swinging lazily open; first one foot emerged, then the other, very gingerly. It reminded him of his grandfather – though this man was barely fifty years old. Titus reached behind his head and deftly undid the straps of the face guard before anyone could stop him. He threw the mask down and smiled. His eyes were the worst thing of all. They were wide and staring.

'Well, well. What a fix we've got ourselves in.'

'Shit . . .' Waites murmured.

'What now?' James whispered, though his words were lost in the rain.

'Why don't we go into the centre?' Titus said; he looked like a zombie. 'We're all terribly wet. Wouldn't want to catch something. Hmm?'

Sean and James exchanged incredulous glances. This was already a situation none of them knew how to handle, but now Titus, or rather the thing inside him, was talking quite normally. They didn't take their eyes off the man as he looked around.

'This is familiar,' he said, taking a step forward. The others all took a step back. Noticing this, the head-master chuckled. 'Oh come on, there's no need to fear me. We can all be friends. Besides, there's three of you and only one of me. I'm not stupid enough to try anything.'

'You'd better not,' Waites said, reminding himself that he was talking to the creature, not the headmaster. 'If we have to kill Titus to get to you, we will.'

'Kill Titus?' The creature smiled again and mulled things over. 'You're really prepared to kill this innocent man? How cold. Although, to be honest, he is already dead: destroying his body will make little difference to him now. As for killing me, well . . . I'm only trying to survive. Isn't that what we're all doing?'

'We don't normally murder innocent people to do it.'

'Survival doesn't discriminate. You do what you have to do. I can't help it, it's something I have no control over. I don't deliberately kill. I have no wish to harm anybody.'

'I don't believe you,' Waites said.

'Me neither,' Sean said. 'What do you want?'

'What do I want?' Titus repeated, as though genuinely considering the question. 'What do I want . . . ?' He was staring at the ground now, but after a few seconds he looked back up at them, smiled, then roared and charged at them, his hands outstretched, grasping for them, murder once more in his eyes.

This time Waites was ready for him. At the last moment he stepped to one side and put out his right foot. The headmaster had no time to avoid it; he flew forward into the mud. Waites rushed across, turned him over and punched him hard in the face. The headmaster was out cold again. Waites undid and pulled off his tie.

'What are you doing?' Sean asked.

'Might be a bit more effective than that face guard.' The teacher wound the tie round the headmaster's mouth twice, securing it behind his head in a double knot. 'There, that should keep the little bastard in there. Come on, guys, help me get him up.'

They lifted the headmaster, this time with Waites taking one arm, both brothers the other, and dragged him along, his feet making two troughs in the mud. They struggled up the hill and onto the pitted road, where they stopped briefly to catch their breath. James looked back at the car: he hadn't locked it, but no one was going to be able to drive it away.

Sean glanced at the tie covering the headmaster's mouth and wondered if it was strong enough to prevent the parasite escaping. They dragged their captive towards the study centre, its lights just visible through the darkness. Sean kept looking at the gag – it seemed to bulge outwards every now and then, but perhaps it was just his imagination.

At the car park they stopped for another breather. Although there were three of them, the headmaster was a large man, and his clothes were heavy with water and mud. When they'd got their breath back, they picked him up again, dragging him into the reception, where a film of water covered the linoleum floor.

They dumped Titus on one of the benches, closed the front door and stood there, panting.

'OK,' Waites said. 'Let's go to Sally's office, James, and try not to drop him ... We don't want him waking up.'

CHAPTER 24

When they lifted the headmaster again, Sean could see that the tie round his mouth was sodden with something dark that wasn't water. It could have been blood, or slime from the creature, but either way it was a bad sign.

James pointed the way along a corridor, past a lecture theatre and two laboratories. Titus's feet scraped along the floor as they pulled him along, a mud slick forming behind him like a snail trail. Sean glanced into the labs as they went by, wondering what would have been going on there on a normal day. A day very different to this one. At the end of the corridor, James indicated a doorway on the right that led to the offices.

'That's it over there,' James said, pointing to a door with a poster of a cartoon Loch Ness monster on it. 'I'll see if it's unlocked.' He went over and twisted the door handle, relieved to find it open. He went in and switched the light on. The room was tidy and clean; there were empty drink cans in the bin, post-it notes with handwritten messages stuck to a computer monitor, and a bowl of fruit, still fresh, on one desk. They dragged Titus inside and dumped him in one corner.

'Sean, you keep an eye on him – tell us if he wakes up or moves. James and I will look for something that might help us,' Waites said.

'OK,' Sean replied, though he wasn't entirely happy with the arrangement. He sat down on a chair and kept his eyes on the headmaster, while he heard papers being shuffled around behind him. He didn't think he'd seen anything as sad, pathetic or disturbing as the man slumped awkwardly in the corner. For the first time he felt genuinely sorry for him. Although strict, Titus had been well-respected, and certainly didn't deserve anything like this. But, like the others, he would soon be dead, nothing but a bleeding mess. When this was all over, when the floods had gone, when the creature had hopefully been destroyed, his family would have to face up to their loss. There would be tears, questions, outrage, but at least he hoped they would be spared seeing him like this. Doing and saying things that were beyond his control. Sean was close to tears himself now. The man before him was dying and there was nothing anyone could do about it. What an undignified end for such a dignified man.

'Shit,' Waites said, throwing random papers to the floor. 'I don't know if this is any good or not. It's just reports and surveys ... How are we meant to know if we've found something?' He looked at James, who couldn't think of anything encouraging to say in reply. He too was sifting through sheets of handwritten and printed notes, looking for a key word or phrase that might be significant. What were they expecting though – an answer written in big bold red letters somewhere, emphasized with a few exclamation marks? It could take hours to go through all Sally Cooper's papers, and then there was her computer. She was bound to have a password-protected user account. The more Waites thought about it, the more Morrow's dying message seemed too vague, too cryptic. If he knew he had seconds left to communicate something, why write something so ... unhelpful?

'Maybe we should try Morrow's office,' James said. 'It's next door.'

'All right. You stay here, Sean. Don't take your eyes off him,' Waites said, pointing at Titus. 'And shout if he wakes up.'

'OK.'

Sean watched them leave the office, and almost immediately felt ten times more vulnerable. The man's hands weren't even tied behind his back. He'd already proved that he could move fast if he had to. What if he had already regained consciousness, and was just waiting for the right moment to attack? Sean shuddered and wheeled his chair away from the inert figure in the corner.

James knew Morrow's office well; his notes were written in a notebook that was kept in his top desk drawer. Morrow only used his computer to access the internet and send and receive emails. When he needed to make notes he always wrote them by hand. James took out the book and flicked through to the most recent entry. Disappointingly, it was four days old and mentioned nothing of the specimen he'd found, which was odd, because James remembered seeing the man writing in a similar book after examining the strange creature. If he'd been writing in a different book, where was it?

'No good?' Waites asked.

'No. It's the wrong one. He definitely made notes about that thing though.'

'Did you ever see it?'

'The specimen? Yeah, but I just thought it was some kind of fish or slug. I couldn't understand why he was so excited about it. He didn't really talk about it to anyone else. Holland must have found out somehow though . . . He was a nutcase. I think it got to him first.'

'So where's this missing notebook then?'

'It could be in his room.' Seeing Waites's quizzical expression James added: 'His bedroom, I mean. Morrow sometimes stayed here when he was working late. A few of the other scientists have rooms here too.'

'All right, we'd better go check it out. Let's just make sure Sean's OK first though.'

They returned to the next-door office, where Titus still lay unmoving. His skin seemed to have broken out in more sores in the brief time they'd been away.

'Any problems?' Waites asked Sean.

'No,' he replied. 'He's still unconscious . . . I think.'

'We need to go upstairs to see if Morrow left his notes up there. Are you going to be OK for a few more minutes?' Waites could tell from the panicked glance towards the body that he wasn't.

'Yeah, but I want his hands and feet tied,' Sean insisted.

'Yeah, you're right.' Waites could now see a black liquid oozing through the gag. It made him feel ill. 'Just need something to tie him up with . . .'

They all looked around the room.

'The blinds,' James said, pointing at the windows. Waites nodded, walked over and started tugging on the long cord, eventually pulling the whole blind down before removing the cord.

'This will have to do. I'll tie it round his hands and feet in one go.' Waites carefully turned the headmaster over, trying to avoid the weeping sores that covered his skin as he did so. He ran the cord round the man's ankles a couple of times, pulled it tight, then used the remainder to bind his wrists, knotting it securely. When he'd finished, he rolled Titus onto his side. He wondered how difficult it was for him to breathe with the tie round his mouth and whatever gunk had collected inside. But there was no way he was removing the gag – he couldn't risk letting that thing out.

'Right. That should do it. Don't take your eyes off him, Sean, and for God's sake don't go near him. We'll be as quick as we can, but if you have any trouble, shout as loud as you can.'

'What if I need to find you?' Sean was looking more and more uncomfortable with the situation.

'Just come up the stairs,' James said. 'They're out here on the left. Just shout for us and we'll come and meet you.'

'Right . . . OK.'

As the other two left Sean looked at the headmaster again; he didn't like being left here with him – he didn't like it at all.

CHAPTER 25

They had only been gone for ten seconds when Sean felt an overwhelming urge to call out to them. So the man was tied up ... So what? The creature inside him was capable of all sorts of things. Sean looked at the tied wrists and feet. Waites seemed to have done a good job, but it might not be good enough to keep the man restrained when he woke up.

A sound that came from out in the corridor interrupted Sean's thoughts. It was an odd scratching or gnawing, and it seemed to be getting closer. He tried to ignore it, but it continued – until finally he had to go and have a look.

He poked his head out of the office doorway; then, when he was confident enough that there was nothing in the immediate vicinity, he stepped out and peered down the long corridor that led past the laboratories and the lecture hall. There was nothing there. The sound had stopped too, so he couldn't tell where it had come from; though as he turned back he heard a new sound, this time a whining – maybe from some lonely or frightened animal in the first laboratory. He knew he shouldn't go any further, that he shouldn't have even left the office, but it sounded like something was in pain, and his instinct was to try and help it.

James led the way up the stairs to the first floor. He had only been up here on a few occasions: it contained sleeping quarters, storage rooms and little else of interest. But he had once gone to Morrow's room to leave him a note about something. He suddenly remembered the doctor was dead; it had completely slipped his mind, and he felt guilty: Dr Morrow had been a friendly, helpful and interesting man, someone James had learned a lot from. He would miss him.

He found the room and opened the door. The bed was made; money, receipts, books and mugs were assembled on top of the chest of drawers. A solitary sock lay on the floor near the bed, and a tiny red light indicated that the TV was still plugged in. A lot of mundane stuff, but considering the owner of the room had been alive until a few hours ago, it all made James feel sad and angry. He walked over to a pile of magazines and notebooks lying on a chair and dumped them on the bed. He and Waites sifted through them, checking each notebook for anything recent. All the notes were old, however.

'Doesn't look like there's anything here,' Waites said.

James dropped the two books he was holding onto the bed and went over to the bedside cabinet. In the top drawer was another notebook, but this one looked new, hardly used. 'Maybe there is . . .' he said.

'Got something?' Waites asked as James flicked to the last few pages of the book.

'I think so.' He read out the last few lines of the last page. '*I am going to wait until tomorrow, then venture outside. I must get away, I must warn everyone about this thing before it is too late . . .*'

The laboratory was cold and a window had been left open so rain and leaves had got in and covered much of the floor and furniture. Nature was invading the building. Sean looked for a light switch and turned all the lights on. The room reminded him of the science labs at school. He couldn't hear the strange sound any more, but he stood still anyway, and waited. Sure enough, after a minute or so he heard something moving at the far end of the room. He went over, stooping to look under the benches in case there was something hiding there. He was almost at the far wall when he saw it. Hunched up in a wet, bedraggled ball was a small dog. It was looking at Sean, its eyes wary, uncertain. Sean approached it slowly now, not wanting to scare it off.

'Hello,' he said. 'Who are you then?'

The dog's ears pricked up, but it stayed where it was.

Sean knelt down and reached a hand forward very carefully towards its head. The dog shrank back a little at first, then moved forward again, sniffing Sean's fingers, then licking them. Sean stroked it, but its fur was wet and smelly. All of a sudden it turned its head as though it had heard something.

'What is it?' Sean asked the animal. 'Did you—?' Then he remembered his responsibility and where he should be and cursed himself for being distracted. 'Come on. Come with me,' he said, then got to his feet and ran back towards the office. He didn't look back to see if the dog was following, but it was. Outside the door he stopped, then went forward more slowly, ready to turn and run at the slightest hint that something was wrong. He inched forward, step by step, wondering if Titus had regained consciousness.

The answer to this, as the rest of the room was revealed, was a clear 'yes'. The second, more urgent question, however, was: where the hell had he gone?

James read the previous two pages of Morrow's diary entries, while Waites stood beside him and did the same. Things had clearly gone seriously wrong at the study centre. The creature had been allowed to progress from a state of harmless dormancy to one where it could manipulate a human being into performing acts of violence; and all the people in the study centre had been murdered by its first host, Holland.

'Are they going to believe this?' James asked. 'The police, I mean.'

'I don't know,' Waites said, shaking his head. 'I'm still not entirely sure I do. This should help though. This and any more notes we can find on Morrow's experiments will help explain things. It still doesn't give us anything we can use to stop this creature though. Why did he try and point us towards Sally Cooper when he died? What was he trying to tell us?'

'I don't know.'

'This guy he mentions in his diary, Holland. Did you know him?'

'Not very well. I saw him a few times around the centre. Bit of an oddball really. Kept himself to himself most of the time. Morrow never got on well with him.'

'Obviously not. Perhaps he knew something about the creature. Where's his room? We should go and see if he kept a diary or made notes.'

'It's just down the hall. Shouldn't we go and check on Sean though? I don't like leaving him on his own with that thing.'

'All right, you go to Holland's room and grab what you can. I'll make sure Sean's OK.'

While Waites headed back to the stairs, James hurried down the corridor. Even before he got to Holland's room he could smell it. It was a pungent composite smell of various elements. Some he couldn't quite make out, but the strongest one was familiar. Blood.

The dog padded into the office, sniffing around and wagging its tail. It circled twice, then sat down and looked at Sean. Sean himself was trying to work out what to do. He went to look around the small foyer between the offices, listening for movement, his heart pounding. Titus could have gone anywhere. The dog started sniffing the damp floor where Titus had been lying, and the discarded cord from the blind. After a second or two it gave a sharp bark, then turned and left the room.

Sean knew he should probably go to look for Waites and his brother, but the headmaster had been his responsibility, and he wouldn't be able to live with himself if he allowed the creature to get away. He headed off after the dog, hoping that Titus had simply collapsed somewhere else, and that he would be able to drag the body back to the office before the others got back from their search.

James pushed the door open slowly; the horrible smell was even stronger now, making his stomach turn. As far as he knew, Holland was the first person to be infected by the creature; Sean had supposedly witnessed his death on the riverbank. If that was true, then the bodies in Holland's room must have been murdered while the creature had been in control of his mind. He paused for a moment, swallowing, then reminded himself that he had an important job to do: this was no time for wimping out.

Important job or not, it was impossible not to be stunned and horrified by the carnage. James guessed that there were the bodies of three people in there, though the number of limbs and lumps of flesh could easily lead one to think there had been more. The carpet was soaked with blood and other matter, and although at first he couldn't work out what had caused the devastation, the long, chewing saw marks in the cupboard suggested a chainsaw. He hoped it was now well away from the wrong hands.

The urge to vomit was powerful but not as strong as James had expected; what he'd already seen had clearly desensitized him to such horror. He approached the desk, which had been damaged by the saw, and noticed the computer monitor. He moved the mouse, flinching as his fingers smeared a drop of blood, and was surprised to see the screen blink into life. The computer had obviously been left on, and as James scoured the desktop icons he noticed one labelled JOURNAL. He double-clicked on it and a word-processing application loaded up. He scrolled down to the last few pages of the document but there were so many mad ramblings and random symbols that he had to scroll back up to find a paragraph that made sense. And what he saw almost made his heart stop.

'Oh my God ... no ...' He re-read the passage, hoping that he'd misunderstood it, but no such luck. It was too much of a coincidence; it had to be real. In which case they were in far more trouble than they realized. He thought for a second or two, then set about deleting the file. It wasn't enough though: he took out his penknife, unscrewed the computer case, removed the hard drive and the screws holding it together, then cut the thin magnetic disks inside to shreds.

When he was satisfied, he tossed the pieces onto the floor and left the room. Thunder was once again reverberating outside and the rain resumed its merciless attack. *This is the end of the world*, James thought. *Who would have believed that it would start here?*

CHAPTER 26

Sean recognized the laboratory as the one in which he and James had found Morrow earlier that day. He hadn't really noticed much back then, but now he stared at all the containers and bottles in the cabinets along the wall, some with coloured liquids in them, others with preserved animal and marine specimens. He thought he saw something moving in one of the large tanks. Since he was already on edge, he decided not to go and find out what it was; instead he went over to the desk and looked through the notes Morrow had left there. He and James had forgotten about these papers. Maybe the answer to Morrow's cryptic message was here somewhere. But he could find nothing that seemed linked to it. Looking down, he saw that the dog had followed him and was now busy sniffing his feet. It glanced up at him questioningly.

'What?' Sean asked. He sighed and looked back at the shelves. He should be tracking down the head-master, but there might be something here, something vital. He scanned the labels on some of the bottles: DISTILLED WATER, RAIN WATER, SEA WATER, LAKE WATER, TAP WATER. Someone was clearly mad about water. Since it was a lake study centre, Sean supposed they did study water here, though he couldn't imagine it made for an interesting job.

All at once he heard a sound somewhere in the laboratory behind him. The dog was still sitting quietly by his feet, so it was something else. He swallowed, realizing how dry his throat had become, and slowly turned round.

In a state of panic, James almost tumbled down the stairs, straight into Waites – who was pretty worked up himself.

'We've got to destroy that thing now!' James blurted out. I don't care how we do it, we have to destr—'

'They're gone,' Waites interrupted.

'What?'

'Sean and Titus. They're not in the office any more. Come on, we have to find them.'

Together they ran down the corridor.

'What were you saying?' Waites asked breathlessly. 'About destroying it.'

'It's worse than we thought,' James said, unwilling to give away too much. 'But just promise me that if that thing gets into me . . . Don't let me out of your sight.'

'Fine.'

'I wish I could tell you what I've just discovered, but the fewer people who know, the better. It narrows the chances of the specimen finding out.'

Waites wondered what that discovery could be, but understood that sharing it could indeed be foolish if he were to become host to the creature.

They were hurrying past the laboratories when they heard Sean scream.

It looked like the parasite was the only thing keeping Titus alive. His skin was an awful translucent yellow pocked with bleeding craters and sores, while the creases around his eyes and mouth had now become cracks that wept openly, the blood more black than red. His eyes were weak and watery and seemed to bulge as though being squeezed by some invisible force. Many of his teeth had fallen out and clumps of hair were also missing. The tie that had once gagged him had long been thrown off along with the cord. He hissed at Sean, his breath giving off a stench of festering, spoiled meat.

'Mr Titus. Are you ... Are you still in there some-where?' Sean asked.

Ignoring this question, the man advanced, still hissing, still fixing Sean with that crazy stare, hands reaching for the boy, for its next victim. Sean backed away, but behind him there was only the whiteboard and the wall; there was nowhere else to run.

'Mine,' the creature hissed again; the smell was atrocious, but Sean was too terrified to feel sick.

'Please, Mr Titus . . .' Sean could hear the quaver in his voice, the terror. Tears were collecting in his eyes now, ready to spill down over his cheeks. 'Please don't do it. Please.'

Titus opened his mouth slowly, and Sean thought he was going to speak. Instead he saw the black, wriggling thing coil around in the ruined mouth, flexing in preparation. Sean was paralysed with fear and unable to defend himself when the creature sprang.

There was a noise like someone hitting a large sheet of metal with a hammer, a clang that went on reverberating. It felt as if someone had attached a sink plunger to his face and was trying to pull it off. Sean fell back against the wall and reached up to try and pull the invader off.

It was too late though. It had already slithered into his mouth, and though the obvious thing to do was bite down on it hard, he couldn't summon up the courage. Then it was at the back of his throat and up inside his head, moving about, finding somewhere to hide. He looked up and saw the headmaster stagger backwards, looking at his diseased hands and then at Sean.

'Oh God . . . What has it done?'

In response, Sean could only shake his head, feeling stunned, almost drugged, unable to do or say anything. He was helpless. The dog, realizing something was very wrong, and not liking the smell of the headmaster one bit, retreated to the other side of the lab to watch.

'Sean,' Titus muttered through cracked lips. 'No . . .' He looked around for something he could use to save the boy, almost whimpering in desperation, already feeling guilty for what had happened. Then he spied the jars of water on the shelf. He squinted at the labels, and almost jumped when he recognized something. He grabbed a jar, re-read the label to make sure he had identified it correctly, then unscrewed the lid.

Sean's vision was changing: Titus appeared to be a great distance away. And sounds were changing too. The drumming of the rain became louder, then seemed to disappear altogether. He couldn't feel his legs and wondered how he was still standing. And all of a sudden, he wasn't.

'Put it down!' came a voice from behind Titus.

The headmaster turned to see Waites and James, the former giving him a stern, angry stare, the latter shocked and deeply concerned.

'Please,' Titus said, not putting the jar down, but trying to placate them with both hands nonetheless. 'It's not in me any more. It's in Sean, but I know how to get it out.'

'Get away from him,' James said, moving forward.

'James,' Waites warned. 'Don't get too close.'

But James wasn't scared of Titus now, just angry. 'I said get away from him!'

'Please, you have to listen. I can get it out of him. Please let me, before it's too late.' Titus held up the jar, but James slapped it out of his hand, sending it flying towards a workbench, where it smashed.

Waites rushed over and looked for the label. When he found it he shook his head. 'Oh God, James, I think he's telling the truth . . .'

James turned, unwilling to take his eyes off Titus, but the headmaster was also looking at Waites.

'Look,' the teacher said, holding up the sodden label. 'Sea water.'

'So?'

'I think that Morrow's dying message wasn't "Sally"; he was trying to write "salt" . . . He just forgot to cross the "t".'

'He must have worked it out during his experiments . . . Or maybe he discovered it when that thing was in his head.'

'Yes!' Titus was nodding, drool dripping from his mouth now. 'It hates it! It can't stand any salt – even the trace salt in the human body almost drives it mad.'

'Well then,' Waites said, eyeing the broken jar. 'Now we have a weapon.'

CHAPTER 27

The revelation was punctuated by a deep and unsettling laugh that came, most unnaturally, from Sean's mouth. In an instant he was on his feet. He kicked Titus in the stomach – which ruptured the man's stomach, spilling blood and matter out onto the floor. Staggering backwards, Titus hit the corner of a bench, cracking his spine and releasing his liquefying kidneys. He sank to the floor in a twitching, haemorrhaging heap. All life was gone from him in seconds.

Sean panted like an animal, then rushed down the aisle between the lab benches, making for the door. Waites was quick to respond and rugby-tackled him to the floor. He knelt on his legs and drew his arms behind his back, incapacitating him.

'James! Quickly, get some more salt water from somewhere. We have to drive it out.'

'What? From where? I—'

'If there isn't any more sea water, find something similar.'

'There might be some saline solution somewhere.'

'That might not be strong enough,' Waites said as Sean struggled beneath him with surprising strength. 'Get some neat salt, and try boosting the saline with that. But hurry, we might not have much time. We've got to get it out of him now.'

James flung open all the cupboards and found both saline solution and sodium chloride. He opened the solution and added nearly a quarter of the sodium chloride, then resealed and shook the bottle, hoping the mixture was well blended. He ran over to where Waites was still battling with his brother, barely noticing the dog, which had come out of hiding and was edging closer.

Waites took the bottle. 'Right, when I turn him over I'm going to sit on his legs. I want you to grab both his arms and keep them down, OK?'

'Yeah.'

'I'll try and get this stuff into him. It's not going to be easy though. Are you ready?'

James just nodded. Waites turned Sean over, fighting to stay on his thrashing legs. James quickly grabbed his brother's arms and forced them down, using every ounce of strength he possessed to keep them there. Waites shook the bottle, then unscrewed the top, and held Sean's lower jaw. The boy's mouth was clamped shut and wouldn't open. A snort came from his nose, and his eyes betrayed the evil monster lurking within.

Waites didn't have time for games. Without any warning, he jabbed his fist into Sean's stomach. As he had hoped, it knocked the wind out of him and the boy's mouth opened. Instantly the liquid went in and was swallowed involuntarily, followed by much coughing and spluttering. There was a delay of a second or two, then the boy's eyeballs started rolling and his body convulsed, making it even harder for them to hold him down. An agonized scream issued from his mouth, then, completely unexpectedly, he threw off the two men holding him down and crawled towards the dog.

James was OK, but Waites had banged his head against a desk in the tumble and was momentarily stunned. They could only watch in shock and exasperation as the thing controlling Sean flew out of his open mouth and straight into the dog's. James got to his feet to grab the dog, but it was off before he could reach it.

Waites looked down at Sean, who was now twitching and foaming at the mouth. 'Take care of your brother, James – I'll go after the dog. If it gets out of the centre it's all over.' Without waiting for a reply, he set off.

Sean looked exhausted after his ordeal. The blow to his stomach still hurt, but it was having the thing in his head that had really shaken him.

James helped his brother into a sitting position. 'Are you OK?'

'I don't know,' Sean gasped. 'My head feels all bloated and ... messy.'

His brother was staring at him, tears flowing down his cheeks.

'James?'

'Yeah.'

'Am I going to die?'

'Don't be stupid. Of course you're not.'

'It was in me though. I mean, that's enough, isn't it?'

'Yeah, but it wasn't in for long though. Maybe ...'

For a while they stayed there, not moving, not talking, too numb to do anything.

CHAPTER 28

Waites knew that tracking down the dog wasn't going to be easy. However, as far as he knew, all the doors were closed. As for the windows, the dog would find it difficult to get through them, even though it was now no ordinary dog.

He moved quietly, listening for any sound that betrayed its whereabouts, checking behind every now and again. He wondered what the creature's plan was. It obviously wanted to survive, just like any other creature on earth, but it was intelligent, so was it planning on doing more than just surviving? If so, what? Now that it was stuck in the body of a small animal, its efforts would surely be hampered. Waites felt sorry for the dog, but if he was able to catch it, he would kill it without hesitation, along with its detestable passenger.

He suddenly heard a sound – a crash upstairs. Something was moving about up there. He went quietly up the stairs, careful not to give away his position. At the top he had a good look around. It was dark, but he didn't want to turn on the main corridor lights in case he startled his target. Creeping forward, his senses on high alert, he wondered what plan the creature had already hatched. If it wanted to get out of the centre, why had it come upstairs?

He padded along the hall until, glancing into one room, he saw that a large bird cage on a stand had been tipped over. Feathers, bird seed and droppings lay scattered around. At first Waites assumed the occupant of the cage was dead, but a flap of wings and a chirp confirmed that the bird was still OK. He peered around the room without actually crossing the threshold. He stood there, listening, barely breathing as he strained to hear the dog. Impatient, he finally went in, switching on the light and looking for clues that it had been there. Suddenly he heard a sound – a loud sniff – from under the bed. Waites was sure it was canine.

'I need to lie down,' Sean said in a weak voice.

'You can lie down all you like soon. First we've got to take care of that thing and . . .'

'What?'

'Nothing. Look, let's get you back to the office. You can sit down and I'll get you some water. Don't worry about what's happened. Like you said, it wasn't in you long; it probably didn't have a chance to infect you.'

But all Sean could do was worry. It wasn't just the taste of the thing lingering in his mouth that bothered him, it was the feeling it had left behind. The feeling of invasion, of control. The thing had wormed its way up into his brain. The thought of it oozing around up there nearly drove him mad. And what of the infection? Was it already taking hold? He would have an agonizing wait to find out.

As he staggered down the corridor after James, Sean's head throbbed, and a horrible metallic taste suddenly overwhelmed his senses. He retched.

'Are you all right?' James asked, stopping.

Sean took a few deep breaths. 'Yeah, I'm fine, just a bit woozy. Come on . . .'

James supported his brother back to Sally Cooper's office. There was still a damp patch in the corner where the headmaster had been lying. Again Sean was filled with pity for him. He hadn't deserved anything like this. He had been put through a terrifying ordeal only to face an agonizing death. At least it had been fairly quick. At least his body had been so far gone that it couldn't fight the inevitable for long. Still, what would Sean say to people who asked what had happened to Titus? What would he say to his family? Assuming he lived to tell anyone anything of course. He slumped in a chair and rubbed his head.

'Do you want me to find you some painkillers?' James asked. 'I think there are some in one of these drawers—'

'No,' Sean said. 'I don't want anything else in my head. I'll just put up with the pain.'

'OK,' James said, wondering what to do next. He wanted to help Waites track down and destroy the dog, but there was no way he was leaving his brother alone. Not now when he really needed him. Then they both heard a cry from what sounded like a long way off, though it must have come from inside the centre.

'What was that?' Sean asked.

'I don't know. Maybe it was Mr Waites.'

Their minds started looking for explanations for the muffled outburst – none were to their liking. Sean looked up at James, and they both knew they had come to the same conclusion. The situation had changed, priorities had altered. If Waites was in trouble and needed help, they couldn't just ignore him.

'Close the door behind me,' James said. 'Here . . .' He opened one of the drawers and produced a key. 'Lock it and don't open it until I come back.'

'How will I know it's you?' Sean asked, taking the key but not wanting his brother to go anywhere.

'You'll know' – James turned and opened the door – 'because if it does get me, I promise you, it won't reach this room.' With that he left, closing the door behind him before he had a chance to change his mind.

Sean, still stunned, rose from the chair and locked the door, shaking more than ever now from shock and apprehension.

CHAPTER 29

Waites knew it was foolish, but he also knew that if he didn't bend down and look under the bed he wouldn't know exactly where the dog was and it might escape. Nevertheless, he did it as carefully as he could. The bedcovers only hung down a couple of centimetres below the mattress, so very little of what was beneath the bed was obscured. But even with the light on, the space there was dark – the animal might charge out towards him with its mouth open. He dropped onto all fours, ready to jump up again, and lowered his head.

All he could see was darkness. He would need a torch . . . Just then he heard the sound again, the sniff, only this time it seemed to come from somewhere behind him. Surely he would have heard the animal move. He stood there, frozen. There was another sound, but not a sniff this time: a low, unfriendly growl just behind his left foot.

Waites turned, and at that instant teeth buried themselves in his Achilles tendon, tearing through skin and flesh. He screamed and reached down towards his foot, only to trip over the dog, which remained clamped to him. He fell and grabbed vainly at the bed for support, landing in an awkward heap on the floor. He gritted his teeth against the pain in his foot as the dog bit down harder. Then he lifted his left leg before slamming the animal hard against the wooden board at the foot of the bed. He heard something break inside it, but its grip loosened only momentarily and its growl grew more menacing. Waites cried out again and took hold of the animal's jaws in an attempt to prise them open – he was terrified that his tendon would snap with the incredible force of the bite – but the dog's jaws wouldn't budge. He kicked the animal against the underside of the bed board, hammering its head until it bled. Finally it let go and limped off, bleeding, out of the room and down the corridor.

Waites had to get up and follow it before it hid somewhere else. As soon as he put weight on his left foot, pain flared all the way up his leg. The tendon was very badly damaged and he would need to get to hospital soon before more permanent harm was done. He looked down at the bird cage and stand, and had an idea: the stand made a pretty good walking stick. He limped out of the room just as James came running down the corridor to meet him.

* * *

Sean stared at the door for a long time after his brother had gone, trying to imagine what was happening. He didn't want to be sitting there, he wanted to be strong; he wanted to be upstairs with Waites and his brother. They would be angry if he left the room, would insist he return, but he would feel better if he went to help them. After all, three would have more chance of finding that thing than two. But at the same time, the odd pain in his head left over from the creature's invasion was holding him back, and that in turn could hold the others back if he went to help them.

But something else was happening right now. The metallic taste had gone, yet something just as distasteful was happening. Images were flicking through his brain like a barrage of missiles, increasing the pain. Most meant nothing to him, making him wonder if it was just his mind reeling from the invasion, but some were familiar. They were like snippets of film. In one he was underwater, looking up at a huge face that looked like Dr Morrow's. The doctor was smiling and saying something that Sean couldn't make out, then reaching down towards him with a huge metal instrument. He was like a giant though – or else Sean was tiny. But the vision was vivid. Sean's hallucinations the day after the race had been pretty real, but these were something new; these were caused by something quite different.

He got up and went over to the window. The rain

hadn't finished with them yet, and the wind was just starting up. Sean couldn't imagine what conditions on the roads must be like now, and how far the floods extended. It would be hell down in the town now, but he would much rather have been a part of that hell than the one he was living here. This was a harder one to explain – a harder one to fix too. He might well not survive this one. If the sickness that had destroyed Dr Morrow, Mr Phoenix and Mr Titus was already in him, working its way around his system, gradually dissolving his vital organs, then he was already dead. Why not go upstairs and fight with the others? Why not take that thing on by himself? If he was already dead, at least he could go down fighting, rather than wasting away in this room on his own.

But that was the problem. He didn't know. He didn't know if he was dying or not, and that confused things. Just then another image came into his mind, and this one really made him pay attention.

CHAPTER 30

'What happened?' James asked, nodding at the blood that had soaked through Waites's sock, shoe and a large patch of his beige trousers.

'It got me, the little bastard. It's like it's rabid, only worse. It went off this way. Look, there's a trail of blood.'

They followed the red drops, James giving the teacher a hand as they went.

'So you hurt it?'

'Well, any normal dog would be lying dead on the floor right now, but that's no normal dog. I've no idea how long it can last with that thing in its brain.'

'God, please don't let it be much longer. How's your foot?'

'My ankle's torn to pieces. It's bleeding badly too. We'll have to stop and bandage it soon, but not until we've sorted this out.'

James looked down at Waites's damaged foot. He was trying not to put any weight on it, and there was a squelching sound coming from his shoe.

They followed the blood trail further down the

corridor, but it was so dark they had to stop and peer down at the carpet for spots of blood. Eventually James was kneeling down to make sure the trail continued.

'Hang on,' he said. 'I think they lead towards that door there.'

They both approached the open doorway leading into a large room that looked like a canteen, with coffee tables, sofas and a small kitchen area at one end. They could see a line of tiny red spots on the linoleum floor, arcing away round a cluster of tables and chairs.

James stepped gingerly into the room and looked for a light switch.

'Be careful,' Waites whispered behind him. 'It's not thinking like a dog any more.'

And as James began pondering the full meaning of these words, his fingers found the switch and flicked it on.

Sean's next vision was from another perspective entirely. He was underwater again, except this time the water was dark and dirty, and he could see particles floating around in it. There was an immense feeling of pressure: something powerful was driving him forward against his will. Then there was light, and clouds and trees passed quickly overhead. With what felt like an explosion of sound and air, his face rose above the torrent and it was like crashing into another, more familiar universe.

He was now moving towards a riverbank, but it was

only a gradual shift, and it seemed a long time before he was close enough to grab tufts of grass to pull himself out of the water. At first he was moving too fast and they slipped from his grasp, but then he was free of the current, and got hold of the bank and pulled himself out of the water, using the last of his energy. His body felt heavy, and there was water in his stomach – foul-tasting water that really shouldn't have been swallowed. But he was out of the murderous river now; he had pulled himself free, perhaps just in time.

He tried to get to his feet, but he still felt so heavy. He had nothing left with which to move himself. Everything had been sapped by the cold water, along with something else; something Sean couldn't quite put his finger on.

The sodden muddy ground shifted beneath his feet now as he dragged himself painfully forward. Then he was looking up, and saw a figure on the muddy slope, blurred by the rain, but definitely another human being. Sean knew the face, but he wasn't used to seeing it like this. It was him – the boy was him – and Sean knew this was no hallucination because he now recognized the situation. It was a memory. Except it wasn't *his* memory.

And as if triggered by this recognition, it suddenly evaporated away from him, leaving the familiar walls of the office.

The spots of blood led past several tables before

disappearing in the direction of the kitchen. Waites and James waited a while, listening carefully, but all was quiet. James looked at the teacher as though awaiting his instructions.

'You go first,' Waites said. 'Sorry, but you're in a better state than me to tackle that thing.'

James nodded gravely at this, then crept slowly forward, tensed, ready to turn and run at any moment.

'I tell you what,' the teacher said behind him. 'There'd better not be any more of these creatures around here . . . or we really are history.' Ahead of him James stopped.

'Er . . .'

'What? What is it?' As Waites drew level with him, he winced at the pain in his foot. It was badly inflamed now, and he could feel the blood still oozing out as he moved.

'You know I found out something when I was in that guy Holland's bedroom? It was a diary . . . I don't know if everything in it was true – he seemed a bit of a messed-up character – but . . . he was always spying on Morrow, reading his notes and trying to interfere in his work. He mentioned something about finding . . . more . . . of these things. Maybe he went back to the place where Morrow came upon the specimen and found others.'

'What?!' Waites shouted, before he could stop himself. They both looked around and listened for any reaction to the noise. 'Why the hell didn't you say something?' he went on more quietly.

'Because the more people there are who know, the

more chance that thing has of finding out. I don't think it knows yet – or maybe it suspects, I'm not sure . . . But if it gets in my head it'll know what I know. It'll know where to find the others.'

'But it was in Holland before. He was the first one it infected. Why didn't it get the information from him then?'

'Well, maybe it did. Maybe that's why it came back here. But if that's true, why is it messing about in here. Why doesn't it just go and find the others? Maybe it was still learning how to possess other creatures, or it could see the others but couldn't locate them . . . Does that make sense?'

'God, I don't know,' Waites replied after a pause. 'It's clearly here for a reason. And if it got into your head, it might be able to locate its mates. Don't tell me anything about their location then. Let's just concentrate on this one; we can worry about the others later. Do you know how many there are?'

'Quite a few, I think,' James said; Holland had used the word *thousands* in his journal.

'All right, we'll worry about them later. Come on, let's find this thing and kill it.'

James moved forward again, his way lit intermittently by flashes of lightning. He had the strange feeling of being in a horror film. Wherever the dog was, it was being very quiet. However, the thing inside it wasn't stupid: it knew its host wasn't ideal, so it was being more cautious now. James remembered Titus's death in the laboratory. The man just fell apart when Sean kicked him, like there was nothing holding his insides together. He remembered too the cold, sickening sensation he'd felt at the sight of that thing wriggling into Sean's mouth. It had been the worst feeling ever. What would happen to his brother now? Could he survive after even those few seconds' exposure? James couldn't bear the idea of Sean having to go through that agony. He knew that if the time came and there was no other option, he might have to—

He shook himself out of his morbid thoughts and tried to concentrate on the task before him. As he followed the bloody tracks, he readied himself to react to any attack. Waites managed to move silently behind him despite the pain he was in.

The drops of blood trailed along the kitchen floor to a space under the counter where there was a pedal bin and a couple of boxes of mineral water. Behind these James saw a glint from what looked like an eye. The dog didn't stir. James kept his eyes on the space, beckoning Waites forward and pointing. He saw him nod, then look around for a weapon.

Waites slowly opened the cupboard in front of him: plates and a jug were all he could see. He tried the cupboard below: saucepans, frying pans and baking trays – much more like it. He chose a heavy iron frying pan for himself and gave James a sturdy saucepan. For a moment he felt ridiculous, but then told himself that they were simply doing whatever they could under the circumstances. They had no access to guns or . . . knives. Why hadn't he thought of that? Although maybe blunt force was the best way to deal with this thing, and swinging a knife around in such a small space might be dangerous. At least with a pan the worst they could do was stun each other.

'Right – how are we going to do this?' Waites whispered, stifling a cry of pain as his foot protested.

'OK . . . I'll charge and scare it out. You hit it.' There was a pause as they both thought this through.

'Can he understand what we're saying?' Waites asked.

James thought about this. The creature had been inside several people now: it had talked through them, used their memories . . . It was now inside a dog, but could it still understand human speech? There was no way of knowing for sure, and they didn't have time to test it out.

'I don't think it'll make much difference,' James said. 'I mean, even if it does know what we're going to do, there's not much—'

The dog chose that moment to dart from its hiding place across the kitchen floor into the rest area. It scampered under tables and chairs, all the way to the windows at the far end.

'Little bastard!' Waites screamed.

Then they heard a thump, and when they turned to look back under the counter, they saw an arm. The hand was greeny grey, and the body it was attached to was surely no longer alive.

'Jesus,' Waites said. 'Who's that?'

'I don't know,' James said after a shocked pause. 'Should I check?'

'You take a look, I'll go after the dog.'

'All right, but don't tackle it without me.'

'I'll just keep an eye on it. Don't be long. Just check if they're alive or not. We'll deal with them once we've sorted the dog.'

Waites moved painfully off after the dog, frying pan held firmly in his hand. James crept over to the storage space and knelt down. The body was that of a young woman in her twenties, though James didn't recognize her. Her eyes were half open, her mouth agape, and James knew she was dead even before he checked for a pulse. She must have been hiding from Holland when he'd gone berserk – though it wasn't clear what had killed her.

Poor thing, James thought. She was attractive, he could tell, even though she wasn't looking too good right now. He was about to stand up when he saw her lower lip move. There was a sound too – air escaping from her lungs perhaps. Maybe she was still alive after all. He put his hands on her shoulders and gave her a light shake. Her mouth opened wider, as if to say something, and that's when the slimy black creature shot out from between her lips and straight into his mouth before wriggling its way up into his brain.

CHAPTER 31

What terrified Sean most wasn't the fact that the creature's memories lingered in his mind, or that he had some psychic link with it; he feared that part of it might have been left behind – which surely made it more likely that he'd succumb to that horrible death. He was staring through the window, unable to move or even remember what he was supposed to be doing, or where the other two had gone. He was stunned, immobile, consumed with dread; he suddenly wondered if it would be better for everyone if he just walked out into the night, never to be seen again.

Then he heard footsteps upstairs and was shaken from his gloom. *No*, he thought, *I'm not going to run. If I only have hours left, I'm going to use them to put an end to all this. I'm not going to die alone and useless.* He felt odd – his stomach ached and he was shaking too, but he walked purposefully out of the office and headed up to the first floor. Whatever task faced him now, he felt equal to it.

* * *

If he'd had time to think about it, James might have wondered why the creature had chosen to hide in the body of the dead girl instead of remaining in the dog. As it was, the alien entity quickly asserted its control over his consciousness. Everything was mixed up in his head – time, names, places – even smells burst from nowhere and confused him, while the creature adjusted everything to its taste. When things settled down again, James was aware only of a smothering darkness; sounds and movement came and went, reminding him that he wasn't asleep or dead, merely locked away in his own mind while something else used his body.

Waites was stalking the dog when James came up behind him. The teacher heard movement under a table and saw the dog limp out, whining and looking up at him as if for sympathy.

'It must be feeling the pain now,' he said to James. 'Bit late to appeal to our better nature though. What do you think we should do – jump on it? Might just squash that thing inside it at the same time.'

He glanced at James, who seemed unusually quiet. 'You OK, James? What about the girl – was she dead?'

There was a pause before the younger man replied, 'Oh, yes.'

'Right, well, you get ready to catch this little bugger if it gets away from me. I'm going to—'

The hand on his throat came as a complete surprise. The crushing power was simply terrifying. He tried to choke out a question, but could do nothing but splutter as he was forced round. Looking into the strange glazed eyes, he tried desperately to escape from the powerful hold. He tried kicking and punching, but this had little effect on his attacker. Waites was sure that James intended to kill him, and that could only mean one thing: somehow the creature had got inside him. Waves of colour swam across his vision and he felt light-headed, but just as he thought he might black out, a strange look came over James's face and he loosened his grip.

Waites broke free and staggered away, nearly falling as his damaged ankle gave way.

'Where *is* it . . . ?' James said impatiently: he was looking at the ground as if trying to remember something. 'Let me see . . . Let me see where they are.'

'*They?*' Waites asked, confused.

But the creature was concentrating hard; it spat in frustration. 'You will show me . . . Or I will find out for myself.' The thing that was James looked up, then turned and marched out of the room, apparently forgetting Waites was even there.

Waites breathed out in relief and limped after it,

wondering how he was going to get that thing out of the boy if there was no more salt water.

Sean was halfway along the first-floor corridor when he saw his brother dart into Holland's room. Hearing furniture being overturned, he came up behind James and saw a mess of papers and books on the bed.

'What are you looking for?' he asked.

There was a pause as James straightened and turned to him. 'We don't have much time. Waites has that thing inside him. He's going to come and try to find out where the others are. We have to stop him or there could be thousands of these things on the loose.'

'Oh my God. It's in *him*?' Sean was aghast. 'Well, we have to get it out!'

'There's no time. We have a bigger problem. We have to find the others.'

'There are more of them? *No* . . .' Sean couldn't believe it. This thing wasn't a single monster, like in horror films. This was one of many, a plague; if the others were just as dangerous, there was no hope for anyone. 'So what do we do?'

'Look through this stuff. See if you can find anything that mentions more of them. There must be something. If we can find it, he can.'

'What about Holland's computer?'

'No good – the hard drive's been destroyed.'

'He destroyed his hard drive?'

'No, *I* did.'

'Why?'

'It had what we're looking for on it.'

Sean sifted through the papers, some typed, some written in an almost illegible hand. He became aware of approaching footsteps and tapped his brother on the shoulder. 'He's coming.'

James looked up at him, then at the doorway. 'Get back,' he said, picking up a table lamp and holding it up, ready to strike the teacher when he walked in.

The footsteps slowed and Sean could tell that Waites was waiting near the door, no doubt aware of them. He looked across at James, whose face was suddenly twisted with hatred.

Then Waites walked in, and everything happened too quickly.

CHAPTER 32

Waites saw Sean first; he was just forming words when James swung the lamp at his head, sending him to the floor. Sean noticed deep red marks on the teacher's neck – the man looked half dead.

James leaped on the teacher's prone body and started punching him, his teeth clenched, spittle flying. Sean couldn't believe it was his brother. Something was wrong. Something was *very* wrong.

Waites struggled and tried to shake James off, screaming all the while for Sean to help him, to stop his brother.

'It's in him, Sean! Get him off me – it's in *him*!'

And all at once things were worse, far worse. Sean was stuck between action and inaction. Part of him wanted to push his brother off the struggling teacher; the other wanted to do nothing and let his brother destroy the creature and the unfortunate body it still possessed. But it didn't make sense. The teacher couldn't move, and the thing inside him would surely have tried to jump into

James's body by now. And James had struck him on the head: that was the weak spot, but Waites was still conscious.

'No!' Sean charged forward into his brother so that he rolled off Waites and onto the floor. He helped the teacher to his feet, praying he had made the right decision.

'Sean,' Waites said. 'We need to restrain him and get that thing out.'

But the creature had already guessed their plan: James was on his feet in seconds. 'It's too late . . . I know where they are.' He turned and ran towards the stairs.

'No!' Sean screamed, suddenly realizing that his brother was indeed infected.

'Damn it!' Waites groaned, rubbing his battered head.

'No!' Sean screamed again in disbelief. 'He . . . He said something about you looking for the others. Lots of them. It must have been looking for them itself though. We've got to get it out of him,' he said, following his brother. 'We have to get it out of him now!'

'We will, don't worry,' Waites replied. 'If it finds the others, we're finished. We're all finished. Come on.'

Downstairs the creature made its way past the lecture theatre and the laboratories towards the front entrance. It only vaguely registered the figure that had once been the headmaster of Orchard Wells High School. Its new body was good. Young, more agile than the others. Strong too. More importantly, the young man's memory had the information it required. He knew where the others were and could picture their location.

It had taken a while to get the information – the boy had been blocking it somehow, but eventually, as the creature had made itself at home, the barriers had come down, and it was allowed access to everything he knew. It could barely contain its excitement. On its own it would only ever be able to jump from host to host. With others of its kind, it could spread throughout the world, using up the humans until there were none left. But there were millions of human beings – it had learned this much. It would take a long time to use them all up. Such fun. And even though it would all come to an end at some point, it would be worth it for the experience, for the education. It would be better than floating around in a pool of water for thousands of years. Lost in its thoughts, it suddenly allowed its host to stumble and fall on his knees, but it didn't mind. In fact it was laughing.

Sean had to help Waites down the stairs: he'd not only been bitten and half strangled, he'd also been bashed on the head. However, they walked as fast as they could – if they lost the creature's trail then all hope would be gone.

They were passing Morrow's office when they heard the front door slam.

'He must have gone out the front,' Waites said, hobbling along. 'Come on, before we lose him.'

Hurrying into the reception area, they opened the front door and peered out into the night.

At first they saw nothing in the dark and the rain. Then Sean noticed something moving along the track leading to the road. James was running down the bank towards the car.

'What's he doing?' Waites asked. 'He'll never get that thing started again – it's finished.'

'He's after something,' Sean replied. 'Maybe a torch.'

'There's one in the glove box. That means we'll need one too.'

'I saw one in Morrow's office,' Sean said. 'A big metal one. I'll go and get it.'

'OK – be quick though. I'll keep an eye on your brother.'

'Right . . .' Sean hesitated. 'Are we going to . . . Will we have time to get it out of him? I don't—'

'We'll think about that later. Right now we have to stop him from reaching the other creatures. What are we going to do about them? If they really are around here somewhere, they pose an even greater threat. We may have to destroy them now while we have a chance.'

'But James – I mean, that thing is the only one who knows where they are.'

'Which means we'll have to follow it and let it find them. For now, just go and get the torch.' Waites gave Sean a gentle push in the direction of the offices.

The teacher couldn't see much, but he kept his eyes fixed on the spot where James had vanished from view. Sure enough, he soon spotted a flicker of light, then James came back into view, running towards the car park.

CHAPTER 33

The creature would have seen Waites if it had turned its head, but it was focused on its objective. It had only seen part of the study centre, but James knew the area well, so the creature was able to combine the mental map in his memory with the information he had read in Holland's diary. It was like having a treasure map and a list of clues. Navigating in the dark would be difficult, but the creature knew roughly where to find the place Holland had mentioned – the place where, after thousands of years of solitude, it might at last be reunited with others of its kind.

James sprinted across the muddy car park, spray exploding around him, and through an open gate into the long grass beside the lake. The torch beam waved around like a searchlight, illuminating the sodden ground and the surface of the lake, which looked alive under the constant downpour.

* * *

Sean retrieved the torch from Morrow's office and would have left immediately had he not noticed something out of the corner of his eye. It was a small Dictaphone, lying beside the slim PC monitor – innocent, lifeless, yet somehow significant. Or was Sean just imagining it? Time was of the essence, so he picked up the small tape recorder and hurried back towards the main entrance.

As he did so, he pushed the rewind button, then depressed 'play'.

'. . . *clear that whatever it is, it is outside our generally accepted evolutionary path. This creature may have been around for millennia, possibly since the dawn of time. It shares characteristics with marine life found in prehistoric waters, but aside from that I am completely lost*—'

Sean stopped the tape and glanced into the first laboratory. A thought had just struck him. He slid the Dictaphone into his pocket and rushed over to the cabinets, trying not to look at the body of his headmaster. He found the shelf with the jars of water, but James had smashed the only one containing sea water. How had James got the creature out of him? It was all so hazy now. Sean looked around and spotted the container of sodium chloride standing on top of one of the benches. Of course.

'Sean!' It was Waites, no doubt eager to follow James. But Sean wasn't ready to do that until he had some way of saving his brother first. He grabbed the sodium chloride, which was now only a quarter full, rushed over to one of the sinks and filled it to the top with water. Screwing the lid back on, he shook it well, then headed back towards the entrance hall.

Waites was growing agitated. 'Come on, we have to go now!' he said as he led Sean out into the wet and dark towards the open gate.

Sean pulled his hood over his head, switched on the torch and held it up, illuminating the path ahead. He could feel the weight of the container in his pocket with the liquid sloshing about inside. Would it work, or would it be too little too late?

'Can you hold this?' He passed the torch to Waites, who took it with a slightly puzzled expression. 'I found this tape recorder in Morrow's office. There might be something important on it.'

'You reckon?' Waites asked doubtfully. 'Besides, you'll be lucky to hear anything in this storm.' He shone the beam round the edge of the lake; on the hillside ahead he glimpsed another light.

Sean took out the Dictaphone and held it to his ear, pressing the 'play' button once more.

'. . . *in trying to find an explanation for it being here. I don't know how it could survive so long unless it has been completely dormant, asleep somehow for millions of years. If so, why wake now? I am sure this creature is*

213

intelligent. It moves cautiously, with deliberation. When I study it I am sure I can see it calculating, predicting. It never acts or reacts instantly. It considers, like a human being would. What if this thing and man are from the same original organism that swam around in the primordial ooze? Could it have evolved to our level mentally, if not physically?

Sean shuddered. The implications of what Morrow was suggesting were sickening. The idea that the creature could think like a man seemed ludicrous, but then hadn't it already shown itself to be clever, devious?

'There!' Waites said, shouting over the din of the rain. 'On that rise over there.'

Sean followed the torch beam and saw the other light, bobbing up and down above the lake.

'There must be a path that leads up away from the water. Come on, this way.' Waites limped off through the mud.

Two questions kept circling around in Sean's head. What if they were too late to stop that thing? And what if they were too late to save James? Tears rolled down his cheeks, but he didn't care. Even if Waites turned round and looked at him, the tears would have been indistinguishable from the drops of rain.

Then, suddenly, the rain abated, then ceased altogether. Sean and Waites stopped for a moment and looked up at the sky, as if waiting to see if it was too good to be true. An incredible silence surrounded them, a strange sense of peace that was horribly misleading.

It was laughing again, but more from the excitement and anticipation than anything else. The exhilaration it felt extended out into its host body, fuelling it with adrenalin, helping it move faster and faster towards its goal. It wasn't too far now – maybe half a mile, then a bit of searching in the darkness. But they were so close now, within reach after so many years . . .

It climbed over a rock and slid down a small slope towards a ditch. It had barely registered the fact that the rain had stopped; it could now just about make out the entrance to the system of caves. It grinned. It inhaled air into its host body and strode forward, never once taking its eyes off the entrance. To think that the others had been so close all this time. The years had clouded its memory, wiped the reason why it had been separated from them in the first place. But it would find out soon enough . . .

CHAPTER 34

'Our closest relation – in terms of intelligence at least. If so ... I really don't know whether to be overjoyed at this discovery or terrified. Considering what it did to the fish, if it can do that to any species it could be dangerous. I certainly don't want to touch it. But what if it could communicate? What if apparatus could be set up to allow it to communicate with human beings? I wonder what it would say ...'

Sean already knew the sort of thing the creature would say if it could talk to humans. And it was nothing they wanted to hear. His boots were now caked with mud, making each step heavier than the one before. Waites seemed to have found a trail that led up the side of the hill. Sean was feeling drained, ill and battered, but he thought Waites must be in a far worse state after being brutally attacked twice. Were they up to the challenge of stopping that creature now that it inhabited a stronger body? And without harming James? If it was to be killed it would have to be forced to leave his body first. That meant getting him to swallow the salt solution.

Suddenly Sean heard the yapping of a dog. He turned back towards the study centre, but could see nothing in the dark. If the dog had survived its ordeal, there seemed no rational reason why it would want to follow them – they hadn't exactly been nice to it. He listened carefully, but could hear nothing more, so he turned and concentrated on following Waites.

It was a hunger now, an insatiable yearning that drove the creature on, pushing its host body ever forward, tripping and sliding in the thick mud several times, but always getting back on its feet, never allowing its thoughts to deviate from its objective. The young man's body moved awkwardly, as if it was drunk, exhausted or on the verge of collapse. When it reached the cave mouth, it didn't even stop to read the warning sign: it just climbed over the thin chain that had been strung across the entrance and stumbled ahead into the darkness, the torch seeking out each nook and crevice. They were here somewhere – but where?

Waites had to stop for a moment to get his breath back. He turned to look at Sean and was about to say something, but changed his mind and started limping off again. Sean could imagine a number of things that Waites might have said, but none would have really helped them at this point. He retrieved the tape recorder and played the last of the message, holding it up now so that they could both hear.

'. . . *but one thing is for certain. This creature, whatever it is, cannot co-exist with other animals. Whatever capacity it has for actual thinking, it does not take even a second to consider the consequences of possessing another creature: it just does it, as if it's natural. With both the fish and Sally's python, it used their bodies to try and escape, assimilated all the information it could, then departed, leaving behind a corpse. Either it is incapable of understanding morality, or sympathy, or it just doesn't care . . .*'

If Waites had heard it all, he didn't give any indication. Sean put the Dictaphone back in his pocket and waded on through the mire. Once over the rise, they stopped briefly to look for signs of the creature's progress. At first they saw nothing: the countryside around them was pitch black . . . then there was a flicker ahead of them. Waites shone the torch towards it and they saw a dark opening in the rock face.

'Must have gone that way,' Waites said.

'Do you think they're in there?' asked Sean.

'Must be . . . At least, it believes they are. But what if this Holland guy was wrong?'

'Doesn't matter. We have to catch it either way. And

I've got to save James,' Sean replied as he turned to walk on.

Waites caught up and took his arm gently. 'Sean ... you know ...'

'I know. But we have to try.'

They shared an agonized look, then went on towards the cave. Sean's boots were really heavy now, and each step was sapping his strength. He was beginning to wonder if he was actually up to fighting the monster, fighting for his brother's life.

The creature had no concept of fear. Its natural sense of self-preservation made it cautious, but it didn't feel the apprehension that a human might: it didn't have the imagination to foresee hidden dangers. So as it made its way through the dank cave, it didn't wonder what might be lurking in the shadows, didn't question the source of the strange sounds; it just went on searching for its goal. It stopped and swept the torch beam around the cavern walls. There didn't seem to be an exit. It must have taken a wrong turn somewhere. It backtracked to a fork, this time taking the other path. Somewhere around here, somewhere close perhaps, were its kin, others that would help it spread through the human race and then the rest of the animal kingdom like wildfire, until there was nothing left.

* * *

Not too far away, the creature's pursuers stepped cautiously into the mouth of the cave, listening carefully.

'Have you been here before?' Waites asked Sean.

'No – but James might have.'

'Well, it could be dangerous, so watch your step.'

'How will it know where to go? This cave system could be vast.'

'Maybe it found a map . . . Or maybe it's a small cave. Either way we'd better catch up before we get lost. Come on.'

Waites moved the torch beam around the cavern until he was sure of the way. There were a number of small openings set into the wall, but luckily only one proper passage. They advanced, and as they did so, Sean reached into his pocket and made sure the solution was still secure. It was the only chance they had of getting that creature to leave James's body. If he lost it, that was it. Waites stopped up ahead and shone the torch around again.

'What is it?' Sean asked.

'I think there are two passageways here. It's hard to tell . . . We'll just have to eliminate them one by one.' Waites led the way into the left opening. They were only a few paces in when he cried out and suddenly the rocks dropped away beneath them. Sean scrabbled frantically for something to hold onto, but it was too late – he was falling through thin air.

CHAPTER 35

The creature had entered a large round chamber. When it shone the torch ahead, strange patterns danced across the wall as the light reflected off a pool of water. It stood by the edge, looking down into the dark water through the young man's eyes. Was it a trick of the light, or was there something moving down there?

Suddenly there was a crash from above, and it seemed as if the whole ceiling was falling in. The creature turned and looked up to see rocks and a body tumbling down towards it. The figure landed with a thud, winced, then looked around, startled. The creature watched as the cloud of dust settled, then turned back to the pool. There really was something moving in the water. In fact, there were a lot of things moving . . .

Waites had managed to get hold of a ledge of rock and avoid slipping down the treacherous, rocky slope towards the cave at the bottom. He hadn't been able to grab Sean though; he swung the torch beam frantically around the sloping tunnel, but there was no sign of the boy. He couldn't tell where the slope led to, or how long it was, but Sean might still be alive: he had to reach him fast.

He retraced his steps, hobbling painfully over the loose rocks and was soon back at the fork. The other passage was narrow at first, but it soon widened out. He hobbled along as fast as he dared, aware that there could be another collapse, shutting his mind to the pain in his foot. If Sean was injured or worse, it might take a very long time for rescue to come – and he had other more pressing problems ...

The creature was aware of the boy scrabbling about in the rubble, panting, cursing and trying to get back on his feet, but all this was only on the periphery of its consciousness. It couldn't tear its gaze away from the black shapes swirling beneath it. There were so many of them, swimming under and over each other. Tens of thousands perhaps. It knelt down and reached out to touch the surface of the water. Gradually it became aware of sounds, voices even, all talking at once, saying the same thing ... although the meaning was unclear. Perhaps the language was unfamiliar because of the time the creature had spent in human minds. And perhaps this odd language had been forgotten over the millennia of separation. How joyous though, how wonderful to finally be here, with so many of its kindred, after so long. The loneliness, the isolation had been appalling. But now all that was at an end. The creature felt like crying with relief.

Sean was in pain – lots of pain. He didn't try to get to his feet straight away; instead he moved each arm, then each leg and foot, just in case something was broken. Despite being banged about and bruised he didn't think he'd suffered any serious damage, so he carefully stood in the darkness. He was shaken, and for a moment had no idea where he had landed, but it was clear it must be some large subterranean cavern. He saw a figure in the distance – could it be Waites looking for him? – and was about to call out when he heard it laugh out loud and realized who it was.

'James.'

The creature heard the name and knew what it meant, but still it didn't turn round. It could feel as well as hear them now. It felt like it was absorbing energy from them – some kind of force that was generated from their mass.

'James!'

Again the creature paid the call no heed. It was so close to its goal now. But suddenly the sense of familiarity was gone and it experienced an odd feeling of disassociation. Now it was actually questioning what it was doing, and what these creatures really were. Had it really been spending too long inside the minds of these human beings? Was its true identity becoming lost? It started to panic. It couldn't allow itself to have second thoughts: this was something it had to do, this was what it had been yearning for.

'James, it's me, Sean . . .' The voice was closer now – it was irritated. But it didn't matter, it could put up with it for now. All those dark bodies down there, all twisting and writhing together. Family. The creature wanted to belong more than anything else, more even than conquering the human race and spreading through them like a virus. It now knew with absolute certainty that it was never meant to be on its own, it was meant to be with them; now it could return to its family for good.

'James, I know you're in there. Please listen to me. It's me, Sean, your brother. You have to fight it.' The voice was right behind it now, and louder than before. The creature was having difficulty ignoring it, its thoughts confused. It could feel the boy, hear his breathing.

'James, please just try—'

The creature turned and pushed the boy over with as much force as it could muster.

Sean went flying across the hard rocky cave floor. He felt his whole frame shake. His back hurt the most, followed by his head, but pretty much every part of him groaned in pain. He looked up to see that James and the thing that controlled him had now turned back to the pool. James was holding his arms up, opening them wide as though ready to embrace some invisible friend. A prolonged gasp seemed to issue from his mouth and he was swaying on his feet, in danger of falling forward into the pool. Sean hadn't actually seen what was in the water, but now he realized that the creature must have found its kin down there. Was it going to free them somehow, let them loose? *This could be the end,* he thought. *Unless I do something right now, this could be the end for everyone.*

He tried to push himself up onto his feet, but the effort required was too great. Most of his strength seemed to have left him. He looked across at his brother in anguish and frustration. Had welts started to appear? He had to do something before the disease took hold. Sean put everything he had into moving his battered body, but as he regained his feet a wave of dizziness came over him and he had to put a hand on the cave wall to steady himself. He tried to focus, and just as he turned to look across at his brother, the worst happened. With a loud, echoing splash of water, it was all over.

Waites was lost. The path had led over jagged rocks and through narrow, claustrophobic tunnels. He could well be getting further and further away from Sean, and if he came to a dead end he might never be able to find his way back. He swore and decided to carry on for another minute or two before turning back and finding another way. Suddenly, in the distance, he heard an awful scream. A cry of denial, of horror. He stopped to listen, but it wasn't repeated, and he had no idea where it had come from. He walked on, praying he was on the right track, but stopped when he heard another noise behind him somewhere – a movement. Something had disturbed the rocks. He turned and shone the torch into the darkness, hearing his breathing quicken. Nothing. *Must be that dog*, he thought. *Must have tracked me all the way down here.*

Sean rushed towards the water's edge, ignoring the protests of his muscles. When he reached the pool he picked up the torch his brother had dropped and was awed and repulsed to see the teeming mass of black creatures, so numerous and so animated that he was reminded initially of television static. Of James there was no sign, and despite the overwhelming urge to do something to save him, he could only gaze at the pool of death from which his brother would surely never return.

But just then a hand reached up through the surface of the water, scrabbling for the rock. It was followed by the head, hair dripping, eyes bulging, with several black, wriggling creatures squirming all over it. Sean could see the desperation in his brother's eyes. He dropped the torch, reached down and grabbed both his brother's hands, pulling him up with every ounce of strength he had left, until they both lay gasping on the floor of the cave. Immediately Sean began to help James tear off the slug-like things and throw them back into the water. James was spluttering w ith horror. 'Get off! Get off me!' Finally his body was free of them.

Sean retrieved the torch and pointed the beam across at his brother, who now lay staring at the ceiling, slowly shaking his head.

'James?' Sean asked. 'Are you OK?'

'I remember now,' James said, looking beaten, dejected. He was shaking and crying. 'I remember all of it.'

'Remember what?' Sean asked.

'They're not like me. Not one of them.'

Sean was confused.

'They have no interest in power . . .' James growled angrily. 'Why must it be like this?' He turned to Sean with open, searching eyes. 'If only they could see how I see, then this world could be ours. How can they possibly be content here, in the dark, for all this time?'

'Sean!' It was Waites's voice. Sean turned to see him limping over from the other side of the cavern.

'Pathetic,' James said. 'Every one of them.' Suddenly he sat up and roared at Sean, reaching out to grab him. Sean knew he had to act fast. He pulled the container

229

of liquid from his pocket, screwed off the lid, then rolled onto his brother's body before he could react, and poured some of the liquid into his mouth. He clamped one hand over James's lips, the other pinching his nose, and forced him to swallow. James bucked beneath him, his eyes bulging as he easily pushed his brother off. He was soon able to get to his feet, where he stood coughing and retching.

Waites approached him, mouth open with horror, but before Sean could shout out a warning, the black creature, covered in a fizzing white foam, shot out of James's mouth and landed on the teacher's face before forcing its way inside. Almost gagging with revulsion, Waites tried to bite down, but the creature's body was as tough as leather now. Somehow it had adapted: it had learned to survive. In no time it was sliding and squeezing its way through the man's sinuses and up into his brain.

CHAPTER 36

'Run! . . . *Run!* . . . *Run!*' The echo continued to travel through the network of caves as Sean and James moved away from Waites's body. Sean had the torch now, and he took his brother's hand as they made their way through the passage Sean had seen Waites emerge from earlier. James was still gagging and spitting salt water as they went, his head pounding, his vision blurred and his thoughts in chaos.

'Sean—'

'Come on, we have to move. What happened in there? In the water?'

'It wanted to join them.'

'So what went wrong?'

'They weren't interested.'

'Why?'

'Because they exiled it thousands of years ago. They cast it out because it wasn't like them. It was bad. But I don't think it's going to be bothering them or us for much longer though.'

'Why?'

'I think it's dying. It's been exposed to too much salt.'

'That mixture I gave you?'

'No.' James spat again. 'It had already taken a lethal dose in the pool.'

'The pool was salt water?'

'Yes. I think that's why it had such a reaction to salt before. It associated it with the rest of its kind and what they did to it.'

'Did you say they "exiled" it? How?'

'I'm not sure. It couldn't remember. It was so long ago. But I sensed the thoughts of some of them. I got the impression it was like a criminal and they had to remove it to stop it poisoning the minds of the others. That's why it was found alone in a separate pool. They found some way of casting it out.'

'And it was hoping they'd join it in taking over the world?'

'Yes. But instead they gave it death – the punishment for returning.'

'So why did it jump to Waites if it was going to die?'

'Because it's angry. It wants someone to blame, someone to punish. So it's going to punish us. It's going to do as much killing as it can before it dies—'

And then, perfectly on cue, they heard a dreadful roar from somewhere behind them, like that of a feral beast.

'But what about the disease?' Sean asked. 'It was inside you for so long.'

'Maybe the salt does something to it. We're both still alive, aren't we, with no lasting after-effects? Let's worry about that later.'

'What about Waites?'

'Well, I don't know. If we can get that thing out of him he might be OK, provided it doesn't make him fall to his death or get lost for ever down here. But that's the problem: even if we survive, we still have that creature to worry about. It won't stop until it kills us or kills itself.'

'How do you feel now?' Sean asked as they stopped at a junction to decide which way to proceed.

'I feel like death.'

Waites – or more accurately, the thing inside him – felt so angry, so resentful and so cheated, that it wasn't thinking clearly. It wasn't taking enough time to make rational decisions. It felt the increasingly agonizing pain from Waites's ankle, but it kept on running regardless. It knew it didn't have long now. It had discovered far too late that the beings it had dreamed about for so many years were not really like it at all. They were the same species, but that was it. They didn't think the same way, they had no interest in power; to them it was an evil force that had to be expelled. The creature was experiencing the extremes of sadness and fury. The cruel rejection had left it feeling more alone than ever. It roared its frustration and tears fell from Waites's eyes as it shook his head. It pushed on, using the man's memories to trace the trail back through the caves, praying it would catch the two brothers before they found a way out. It had plans for them – plans that didn't involve them leaving the caves alive.

Sean had the terrible feeling that the monster was getting nearer. They had taken a couple of wrong turns and it felt like the creature could sense them, smell them. Every now and then they heard its roar, and each time the sound was closer. James bent over with another wave of nausea and was relieved to see that Sean hadn't noticed. Now more than ever he had to be the strong big brother and ensure that they both escaped. The residue of the salt was everywhere – in his mouth, his nasal passages, his stomach. It had probably saved his life, and yet the creature's hatred of it must have lingered, as it felt like poison in his system. He spat out a mouthful of salty saliva and pressed on, checking Sean was OK, and then they both felt a cold blast of air and saw moonlight.

It was almost upon them. The faster it went, the hungrier it got, or was it the other way around? It couldn't be sure any more. But it could almost smell the vapour they left behind them as they ran, processing it to gauge their state of mind, their state of health. They would soon be in sight, and it would tear them apart, destroying their world. Just like its own world had been destroyed. Utterly.

It limped on faster and faster, ignoring the pain from Waites's ankle. It hoped that he would die – another victim in its new war. But until that moment, until its host collapsed, it would destroy every bit of life it could find.

The fields around the lake and the cave system were now almost completely water-logged. In front of them, the long ridge of high ground had become an island in a vast, shallow sea. In many places the water was only a few centimetres deep, but in the darkness it seemed like they were looking out over a huge black ocean. How had things got so much worse in the time they'd been inside the caves?

'Which way is the centre?' Sean asked.

James was about to answer, but then realized that everything looked different; though he knew the general direction of the study centre, he didn't recognize his surroundings. But there was no time for hesitation: they had to keep moving.

'I think it's this way. Be careful though.'

They splashed their way across the small channel and up the rise. From here they could just make out the centre beyond the trees below them. But the path was nowhere to be seen, and they had to slip and struggle their way down the muddy slope.

'How are we going to get back to town, James?' Sean asked his brother. 'Waites's car's wrecked, isn't it?'

'Yeah, we'll have to take one of the others at the centre.'

'Do you know how to hotwire them?'

'What? Of course I don't. There's a car that belongs to the centre that people borrow from time to time. I noticed it earlier. I'll get the keys from reception.'

They pushed on, unaware that their pursuer was already emerging from the mouth of the cave.

Sean's shoes were full of water – there wasn't a dry patch of material anywhere on his body. He was shivering and fantasizing about being dry and warm at home. He cast his mind back to that morning, lying in bed, stir crazy. It seemed like days ago.

They splashed across the car park and into the study centre. James went behind the reception desk and retrieved the key.

'Here we go. Right, come on, let's get out to the car. I don't know how we're going to get back to town, but we'll manage it somehow,' he said.

They staggered back out into the night.

'The car's over there,' James said, pointing. 'I hope it works – it'll need to—' He stopped dead.

Waites was standing in the middle of the car park, staring directly at them, his expression showing both pain and fury, his hands clenched by his side. The brothers were rooted to the spot in terror.

'Sean . . .' James said, turning the keys over in his hand.

'Yeah,' Sean whispered back, trying not to move his lips.

'When I say "go" . . .'

'I don't know if I can.'

'You have to.'

They could hear Waites's breathing now – almost a hiss – but he just watched them, waiting for them to make the first move. Then he spoke.

'You think you've won . . .' The unfinished sentence hung in the air, then: 'But it's already over. Don't make it difficult.'

'Look,' James replied. 'We just want to get home.'

'Yes!' There was a laugh. 'Home. You have a home. What joy.' It came towards them now. The two boys tensed, ready to run, but it stopped again. 'I had a glimpse for a while. A glimpse of what home meant. To belong, to be safe and loved.' A shake of the head. 'I don't hate you because of what you are, because you're different to me. I hate you because you're happy, because you are not alone. Because you have everything that I do not. And while others of my kind may feel guilty, ashamed of such feelings of jealousy and hatred ... I do not.'

'That's right,' James said. 'That's why they cast you out. You're a freak, a monster ... Even to them.'

'Yes.' It was smiling now. 'A monster ... That's exactly what I am.' Then it looked up, opened its mouth and roared, charging towards them ... And all at once everything shattered.

CHAPTER 37

Even as they ran for the car, Sean glimpsed the showers of water sent up by the monster. The sound that came from its lungs was horrible, unearthly. James scratched the paintwork of the car door in his hurry to get the key in the lock: the monster was coming for them, eager to murder, to destroy.

James opened the door, got inside, then realized he had to stretch across to open Sean's side. Looking up, he saw that Waites was almost upon his brother.

'Sean!' James reached for the door, but it was already too late. Waites launched into his brother, slamming him against the car with a sickening crunch. Sean collapsed like a sack of potatoes. James watched in horror, screaming inwardly as what had once been his teacher picked up his brother's body and flung it up into the air; it crashed down into a puddle and lay still.

The monster turned to face the car once more and growled. James locked his door and put the key in the ignition, feeling sick to his stomach: how was he going to retrieve his brother and escape? He turned the key and the car started. The creature banged furiously on the roof, incensed at being deprived of its prey. Suddenly the glass of the passenger window shattered, but the car was moving now. James brought it round to where his brother lay.

The monster watched and shook its head. How could these creatures be so stupid? How could they risk their lives so selflessly? They didn't appreciate the importance of self-preservation. It would simply kill them both now. Surely one of them escaping alive was better than neither. That had to make sense. But the older brother hadn't just driven away. He had stayed. What utter stupidity.

The monster marched over to the car, shaking his head and wishing that the end could have been more of a challenge.

Sean was drifting in and out of consciousness. One moment he was underwater, bobbing along with the creature's memories; then he was in the office, guarding the headmaster's body; then watching Titus's stomach explode; then he was seeing his brother plunge into the pool, consumed by several thousand wriggling black creatures. He felt everywhere and nowhere. He opened his eyes and saw a night sky, darkness. His body felt twisted, broken. His head pounded, his heart beat madly in his chest and there were stabs of pain when he breathed. Blinding light now, and the sound of an engine.

James knew he had to get out of the car to help Sean, and the sooner he did it the better. If the monster couldn't reach him, it might attack his brother again. He opened his door and climbed out, running round to where his brother lay. He knew that moving him was a bad idea, but there wasn't time to be careful. There was the yapping of that dog again – the one that had been in the centre. James realized that the monster was only metres away now; he looked down at his brother. Sean's eyes stared up at him, then flicked down towards his left hand, which held something that protruded from his coat pocket.

'The only way . . .' Sean gasped weakly. 'It's all we have.'

James took the container and stood up. The little dog was barking at the creature, challenging it. James turned the container over in his hand and wondered how on earth he was going to do what he had to.

In no time the creature was right in front of him; it slapped the container from his hand, sending it flying to land in a puddle. It then gripped James by the neck and hoisted him into the air.

James choked and struggled; he kicked his legs out at his attacker while his hands tried to free the grip on his throat. But the monster's strength and determination were too great.

Yet even as it squeezed the life from him, something

shifted in the body it inhabited. So far it had managed to contain the feeling of pain from the ankle. Now though, with the added stress, Waites's foot was rending, tearing. The creature groaned and staggered backwards, closing its eyes to block out the agony. Out of nowhere, the dog rushed in and sank its teeth into the wound it had opened earlier.

The monster screamed and tried to shake it off, but the little dog was clamped on with all its strength, made all the more determined by the noise. It began moving its jaws from side to side, destroying the already torn ligaments of the ankle. And then, suddenly, the ankle gave way completely; there was a crack as the bone fractured. The dog darted out of the way as the monster collapsed, releasing its prey.

There was a splash followed by more cries, and James lay there, massaging his neck and gasping for breath. He could see Waites's foot – it was seriously damaged if not destroyed. There was no way that thing would be chasing after anyone now. He glanced around for his brother, and was surprised to see him crawling towards the monster, which was still writhing and crying out in agony.

'Sean! Keep away from him!' James could do no more than gasp; he doubted his brother could hear him over the screams of agony. Sean's face was a mask of pain and exhaustion, but he crawled on – and James suddenly glimpsed the bottle in his hand.

'Careful . . .' he whispered, feeling like he might pass out at any second. 'Be careful, Sean.' Watching was all he could do now, much as he wanted to help finish off that awful creature.

As Sean twisted the top off the container, the eyes of the host fixed directly on him. The creature growled.

'You have no hope. There are more of my kind, thousands more—' It broke off and roared again in pain.

'Yes, I know,' Sean said weakly. 'But they're not like you.' And he poured the remaining liquid into the open mouth, clamping his hand over it and holding the nose. There was a convulsion as the creature tried to disgorge the salt water, but it was forced to swallow the toxic liquid. It thrashed around in pain, then flung out its arms and pushed Sean away.

'You'll all die,' it spat as it sat up. 'Every single one of you miserable creatures.'

Then Waites's mouth opened wide and the black slug emerged like a snail from its shell. It was foaming and hissing from the salt. As Sean and his brother watched, it oozed out and plopped onto the wet ground, where it curled itself up into a ball. The salt continued to eat away at it, turning it to liquid. Almost casually, the little dog trotted up to it, sniffed it, then started idly chewing it to pieces. It soon decided that the salty treat wasn't such a treat after all and let it fall into a puddle, where it lay still.

Sean crawled over to James and slumped down beside him. 'James?'

'Yeah,' his brother croaked.

'We'll never make it home like this.' Sean was surprised to hear his brother attempt a laugh.

'No, you're right. We won't.'

'You know what?'

'What?'

'I wish I'd stayed in bed this morning.'

Now they both laughed and James managed, with no little discomfort, to put his arm round his brother. For several minutes they just sat there, leaning against the car, hoping the rain really had stopped.

'What's that game you got the other day?' James rasped. 'The one with the zombies in it?'

'*Undead Platoon*,' Sean told him. 'Why?'

'Fancy a game later?'

'Yeah, sure.'

'I won't beat you too badly.'

'Won't beat me at all.'

'Yeah I will.'

'Nope.'

'Yep.'

Sean shook his head.

James nodded his and they both laughed again.

EPILOGUE

The study centre was quiet when morning finally came. The birds had emerged from hiding and were filling the air with their raucous song. The electricity was still working and the two brothers were able to find a couple of heaters to warm themselves and dry their clothes. They'd bandaged Waites's foot as best they could, but it was in a terrible state. James was no expert but he thought the teacher might have to lose it. They'd given him painkillers, fed him, washed him and put him to bed. Then they'd showered and found some food in the canteen. Their fatigue got the better of them: even though they had intended to leave the centre at first light, they soon collapsed on a bed, drifting very quickly into a deep sleep.

When they woke it was almost lunch time. They ate again, then agreed that they should wait until the waters had receded significantly before trying to get back into town. The land lines weren't working, and James's mobile phone showed only a very weak signal, but he had managed to send his mother a text before he lost it altogether. As long as their parents knew they were safe, they could stay at the centre for a while longer if necessary.

Incredibly, by late afternoon the water level had dropped dramatically and though most of the surrounding fields were still waterlogged, the roads looked passable. Sean and James gazed out at the landscape from the first-floor windows before deciding it was worth a try.

James went to check on the patient. Before his mobile signal had disappeared, he'd wanted to call for an ambulance, but Sean quite rightly pointed out that even if one were available, it would never have been able to cross the bridge in town. Waites was still asleep. They didn't like the idea of leaving him in the centre on his own, but moving him sounded like a worse idea. The salt water seemed to have banished the infection left behind by the creature, but he'd been in serious pain, and his ankle would get infected if it wasn't treated quickly. They would contact the police as soon as they got home and make sure Waites received medical help. If the emergency services were too busy, then they would return themselves.

'What's it going to be like down there in town?' James asked as they got into the study centre car.

'I don't know,' Sean replied. 'Wet?' They both smiled.

'I wonder where that dog got to,' Sean said, looking around.

'Don't know,' James replied, easing the car towards

the road. 'No idea where he came from either but I'd like to shake his paw.'

Even though the floodwater had receded, there were still large stretches of water across the road, and James had to drive slowly and carefully through each one. By the time they reached the school, still quiet and abandoned, it felt like they'd been driving for hours. James took it steadily down the steep hill towards the town. A roadblock had been set up near the market place, and a stern-looking police officer told James he could drive no further, then immediately went off on other urgent business. James decided to park the car by the nearby supermarket.

The town seemed so different now. Everything was darker, dirtier than they remembered. The trees by the river seemed to have lost their lustre, and one or two of the buildings looked like they were on the verge of collapse.

They stopped by the bridge and were disheartened to find the river still surging just below the road itself. Police tape had cordoned off the bridge, but there were no officers around, so the two brothers slipped under the flimsy barrier and ran across. Once on the other side, Sean glanced back across the water to see the drenched, dishevelled figure of Mrs Rees being comforted and guided towards the high street by two police officers from the direction of the park. She had clearly survived: if she had been infected, she would have been dead by now. The two brothers smiled as the poor woman was helped along, clearly the worse for her ordeal but alive. They headed away from the bridge and in no more than ten minutes they were home.

They phoned the police and tried to explain about Waites and what had happened, and why he was in the study centre on his own. There was a lot more explaining to do, but that could come later. Right now there were urgent problems to deal with. Several people were still missing since the start of the flooding. Three buildings had collapsed into the river, and many more were swamped by the filthy floodwater.

Sean's mum stroked his cheek before he turned to go up to his room. Even though both he and James were sure that the creature's infection wouldn't do any lasting damage, they would have to get themselves checked out at the hospital as soon as possible. They both had an odd red rash that must be a side-effect – though it caused no pain or discomfort.

'What on earth happened to you, Sean?' his mum asked as he started up the stairs. 'Are you still ill?'

'I don't know,' he replied, stopping halfway up and thinking for a second. 'I think there might have been something in the water.'

ACKNOWLEDGEMENTS

I would like to thank Harriet Wilson for editing, and Sophie Nelson for copy-editing this book. Their hard work and enthusiasm is most appreciated. I would also like to thank my long-term editor, Charlie Sheppard, for her continued support and wisdom.